find me a boyfriend, Jared,

Sharlie said. "It's been weeks since you said you'd help me."

Jared rose and crossed to the fireplace, his thoughts tucked behind the neutral expression on his face. "Still interested in a brief affair?"

Sharlie was momentarily stumped. She sensed a judgment lurking behind that question, but Jared's voice was as even and cool as the look on his face. The truth was that she wasn't sure what she wanted anymore, but some perverse part of her made her answer in the affirmative.

"Yes, I think brief would be best, a good way to start...."

"What about love?"

"I tried it, it didn't work out. If it happens, it happens. If not..." She shrugged again.

Jared scowled at her. "Don't be ridiculous, Sharlie."

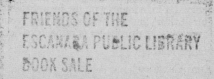

Dear Reader,

It's May—spring gardens are in full bloom, and in the spirit of the season, we've gathered a special "bouquet" of Silhouette Romance novels for you this month.

Whatever the season, Silhouette Romance novels *always* capture the magic of love with compelling stories that will make you laugh and cry; stories that will move you with the wonder of romance, time and again.

This month, we continue our FABULOUS FATHERS series with Melodie Adams's heartwarming novel, *What About Charlie?* Clint Blackwell might be the local hero when it comes to handling troubled boys, but he never met a rascal like six-year-old Charlie Whitney. And he never met a woman like Charlie's lovely mother, Candace, who stirs up trouble of a different kind in the rugged cowboy's heart.

With drama and emotion, Moyra Tarling takes us to the darker side of love in *Just a Memory Away.* After a serious accident, Alison Montgomery is unable to remember her past. She struggles to learn the truth about her handsome husband, Nick, and a secret about their marriage that might be better left forgotten.

There's a passionate battle of wills brewing in Joleen Daniels's *Inheritance.* The way Jude Emory sees it, beautiful Margret Brolin has stolen the land and inheritance that is rightfully his. How could a man as proud as Jude let her steal his heart as well?

Please join us in welcoming new author Lauryn Chandler who debuts this month with a lighthearted love story, *Mr. Wright.* We're also proud to present *Can't Buy Me Love* by Joan Smith and *Wrangler* by Dorsey Kelley.

In the months to come, watch for books by more of your favorites—Diana Palmer, Suzanne Carey, Elizabeth August, Marie Ferrarella and many more. At Silhouette, we're dedicated to bringing you the love stories you love to read. Our authors and editors want to hear from you. Please write to us; we take our reader comments to heart.

Happy reading!

Anne Canadeo
Senior Editor

MR. WRIGHT
Lauryn Chandler

Silhouette
ROMANCE™
Published by Silhouette Books New York
America's Publisher of Contemporary Romance

For my parents, Laura and Barney Chandler Warren,
who make all things possible.
And for Tim, who makes romance real.

SILHOUETTE BOOKS
300 East 42nd St., New York, N.Y. 10017

MR. WRIGHT

ISBN: 0-373-08936-8

First Silhouette Books printing May 1993

All the characters in this book have no existence outside the
imagination of the author and have no relation whatsoever to
anyone bearing the same name or names. They are not even
distantly inspired by any individual known or unknown to the
author, and all incidents are pure invention.

®: Trademark used under license and registered in the United States
Patent and Trademark Office and in other countries.

Printed in the U.S.A.

LAURYN CHANDLER

has wanted to be an actress since she was seven. Her parents suggested that she establish a secure career to "fall back on," so she decided to become a novelist, too. She finished her first book when she was fourteen—a very *long* story about a San Fernando Valley hockey team and their dying goalie, who happened to be a woman. "I figured I could play the lead when the book was made into a movie," she remembers. After graduating from U.C. Irvine, she became a waitress with dreams of glory. One day, she wrote another book, sent it to Silhouette, and, as she puts it, "Here I am, doing what I love!"

AUNT ESTHER'S
COCONUT-CHOCOLATE BAR ICE CREAM

4 cups milk
1½ cups sugar
4 eggs, separated
1½ tsp vanilla
2 cups whipping cream
1 cup flaked or shredded coconut
½ lb bittersweet chocolate bars, broken into pieces

Combine milk, sugar and egg yolks in double boiler over medium heat. When the mixture reaches a soft-custard consistency, remove it from the heat. Add vanilla. Beat the egg whites until soft peaks form and fold into custard. Whip the cream until soft peaks form and fold into custard. Gently stir in coconut. Freeze according to the instructions for your ice-cream maker. Add the chocolate toward the end of the freezing process. Binge!

Chapter One

Blurp.

The last drop of frosting sputtered hesitantly out of the pastry bag and landed with a plop on the side of the cake. It didn't look like a rosette.

Charlene Elysia Kincaid dropped her head and groaned in frustration. Her eyes lowered to avoid the sight of the blob, and her hand clenched to squish the pastry bag that made it.

"Damn!" Tossing the bag onto the counter, Sharlie straightened and shook out her shoulders. Tension crept along her neck and down her spine, and she winced. She had been bent over that cake for four hours now—four whole hours of frosting and piping and making it beautiful.

"Not *beautiful*," Sharlie corrected herself firmly, "*perfect*. Concentrate on perfection." Birthday cakes could be beautiful. Cakes for anniversaries and Bar Mitzvahs could slide by on mere beauty.

But not this cake.

She stepped back and studied her work. Behind tortoise-rimmed glasses, her gray eyes were critical as they roved over the fourth and final tier of the cake, searching the elaborate princess design to uncover the slightest margin for improvement. This cake would be special, a creation....

"Lotty!" Sharlie jumped forward as a tiny Siamese kitty popped onto the counter, making rapid progress toward a cake inspection of her own. Sharlie lifted the cat without delay, ignoring the indignant meow as she tucked the furry creature under her arm. The small, pugnacious face glowered up at her.

"Tough luck, cat," Sharlie smiled, bending her head to nuzzle the silky fur of her beloved feline. "I told you, one hair in the frosting, and the Board of Health will have Aunt Esther's food license. And you, my sweet little Lotty, will be cat stew."

"I don't care about the Board of Health, if it's the business you're worried about," a voice replied. "And I'd like to put more than cat hair in that oversized cupcake you've been wasting your time on!"

"Aunt Esther." Sharlie looked up at her great-aunt and smiled sheepishly. Iron-gray curls capped Esther's head like a fuzzy steel wool scrubbing pad. Her blue eyes spit anger and sparkled, and her lips thinned disapprovingly as she stared in frustration at her favorite niece and employee. In a suddenly self-conscious gesture, Sharlie pushed a long blond curl from her eyes. A single look from Aunt Esther could make her feel more like a naughty child than a reasonably adult twenty-four-year-old.

"How long have you been standing there?" Sharlie asked, wondering if her face betrayed emotion as vividly as Ester's did.

"Long enough to see that you're making a fool of yourself." Esther's pink face wrinkled unhappily as she glanced at the cake. "You're just being ridiculous, that's all. Decorating that man's wedding cake! Whoever heard of such a thing? It's so... so civilized!" She spat the word out like it had a bad taste.

Of sympathetic sour grapes, Sharlie guessed silently, knowing the flavor well. The taste of sour grapes had been lingering in her own mouth for months, and now—only hours before Glen's wedding—it was stronger than ever.

"How did he talk you into it?" Esther's voice rose suspiciously.

"He didn't talk me into it. He just asked." She handed the cat to her aunt and began to untie the frosting-stained apron that covered her jeans. "Anyway, it's good for business," Sharlie argued reasonably. "You *are* a caterer, and this *is* a party."

"Some party," Esther snorted with unladylike bluntness as she held the squirming cat away from her. "He's marrying the wrong girl. And where on earth did he get the audacity to ask you to supply his wedding cake? What kind of poet doesn't have any feelings?"

"He's a wonderful poet, Aunt Esther!" Sharlie defended Glen so quickly she wanted to kick herself into silence. *That's me,* she thought disgustedly, *loyal Sharlie. I should have been a sheepdog.*

She looked at the wedding cake and sighed. That was the price of love: it turned you into a human puppy, all dewy-eyed and trusting and practically panting for a kind word or a pat on the head. And then, if you got that, you were left at home with the cat while everybody else went off and got married.

Sharlie lifted her apron over her head and turned away from the cake. Esther was starting in on another mini-tirade about the fickle quality of the human heart in general—and Glen's in particular—but Sharlie didn't listen. She was tired, tired of trying not to think about him and tired of being able to do nothing else. From now on she would consider the human heart a purely physical phenomenon.

Love. She wouldn't even be on speaking terms with the emotion if it hadn't been for Glen. Unlike every other normal, healthy young woman in the modern world, she had somehow managed to grow to adulthood without ever having experienced the warm, heady rush of romantic love. She had pragmatically confined her crushes to the occasional television star or movie idol, the untouchables, men she could build fantasies around without having to test her ability to love or to be loved in return.

Apparently there had been a clerical error when the angels were passing out confidence. They'd given Sharlie a double dose of shyness, a too-healthy helping of baby fat, and then had left her to fend for herself where men were concerned. Unfortunately, high school and cellulite simply hadn't mixed. By the time Sharlie had lost the weight and toned up in college, her dating confidence had been sorely undermined. Her lack of experience had made her feel extraordinarily stupid, and the idea of getting experience with someone she did not love had made her feel sick.

And then, when the nunnery was beginning to look better and better, along came Glen, wonderful Glen, a grad student poet, who was filled with all the excitement and panache she had dreamed her Mr. Right would have. He poured his emotion into his poetry, and, best of all, he made her heart race every time she saw him.

Sharlie had listened to his poetry with the devouring ears of a lover. He had examined her artwork with the thorough eye of a critic. She'd made lavish delicacies for him to try, and he had eaten them like...well, like he was hungry. It had been enough for her. She'd never believed that a feeling as strong as hers could have failed to be returned.

They'd graduated and still she'd been content to love him patiently, privately, noiselessly. She had waited so long to be in love, she hadn't wanted to destroy the illusion by pressing the reality.

She would be sitting with him today, no doubt, discussing the effect of alliteration in E.E. Cummings and feeling her heart pound with every glance he gave her, if she hadn't been set straight very firmly and very unmistakably one very long night a month ago.

Every time she thought of that night, she felt a burning in the pit of her stomach that probably meant true love was giving her an ulcer. She shook her head. No, not true love— Jared Wright: he was the one who was making her sick. Sharlie's toes curled with resentment. Her whole body cringed with the memory. That rotten, cynical, skunk of a man. He had ruined what should have been the happiest night of her entire life. He had blackened her future. He had pointed out the truth.

Oh, that night, that night! Would she ever forget that night? She closed her eyes. Nope.

She'd spent all day getting ready for that lousy party, a party to celebrate the publication of Glen's first book of poetry. She could have roasted a side of beef in the time it had taken her to do her hair.

Glen had been away for three months, lecturing at a private college, while Sharlie had beaten egg whites into meringue and thought about him incessantly. Even missing him had made her feel alive. And, finally, she had come to a decision: this party was going to be the start of a brand new life for them. Tonight was going to be different from every night that had come before it—all those stumbling, adolescent nights and days when she'd been too shy or insecure to let Glen know how she felt about him.

After tonight, nothing would ever be the same again.

She'd gotten that part right, anyway.

To prepare for that fateful evening, she'd woven her curls into a herringbone braid; she'd bought a simple floral-print dress that clung to her curves. Over and over she'd imagined telling Glen exactly how she felt. Then she had imagined showing him.

When she arrived at the party, her imagination was flowing as freely as the champagne. She intended to make it easy for Glen to admit that he loved her. And the champagne was going to make it easy for her.

Her first glass traveled the distance from stomach to brain with alarming rapidity. By the last drop of her second glass, her head felt unusually comfortable, as though it were floating somewhere off her neck, and an unfamiliar but very pleasant giddiness claimed her.

If I'm smart, I'll give in, she thought and, reaching for her third glass, she determined to do just that. Her normally shy reserve failed her utterly as she giggled and teased and otherwise flirted with Glen in a manner guaranteed to make his eyes pop from his head. Every word, every gesture she made was a feather to tickle him into boldness.

Unfortunately, by the time she had reached for her fourth glass of champagne, Glen still hadn't displayed much boldness, and his eyes may have widened a few times, but they certainly hadn't popped.

It was a different pair of eyes, the color of amber, and piercing, that alternately narrowed and bulged as she tried her hand at the art of seduction. Jared Wright watched her every move like a hawk on the wing.

Standing on the edge of the party, Sharlie took a welcome break from flirting, which was turning out to be a lot of hard work. Glen had retreated minutes ago to discuss Camus with a lit professor from Utah. Sharlie had lost sight of them. Peering over the rim of her champagne glass, her eyes caught Jared Wright, and she looked at him speculatively.

Tall and imposing, with hair a shade or two darker than his eyes, he was the owner and president of Jarico Publishing, the independent press that was publishing Glen's work. Jared Wright was handsome, but his features lacked the sheer male beauty of Glen's. Glen was so physically attractive that Sharlie's pulse raced with pure nervousness whenever she saw him. Jared's appeal was more approachable, although he conducted himself with an air of natural confidence that was commanding to say the least. Sharlie envied it.

Her own confidence was champagne-induced. Studying Jared critically, she wondered if he had ever suffered a moment of the adolescent insecurity she had dragged straight through into adulthood. Not likely, she decided. She knew the type. He probably dated glossy-haired brunettes with porcelain nails and sandy blondes with perfect tans, women who never had to shop for control-top pantyhose.

And he usually looked right past the Sharlie Kincaids of the world, she acknowledged with a wry grimace. But that was only because the Sharlie Kincaids of the world usually let him.

She generally commanded as much attention as Cinderella *before* the ball. But tonight she refused to fade in with the furniture, and lo and behold—someone like Jared Wright was paying close attention.

I'm clearly a woman who knows her own power, Sharlie thought with giddy abandon. Now if only she could use that power to get what she really wanted. She brought her glass to her lips once more, but it was empty. Sighing, she placed it on a side table and wandered among the guests.

First she found more champagne; then she found Glen. He was standing in the doorway with Jared. Both men had genial smiles on their faces, and Sharlie felt her heart go soft as she looked at her handsome poet next to his publisher. Glen and Jared moved farther into the room, and without allowing herself to think twice about it, Sharlie leapt into action.

Armed with her champagne, she sidled up to Glen, linking her arm with his and, in a totally uncharacteristic maneuver, wiggled her other arm around Jared's.

Jared Wright's dark eyebrows rose, and his lips curved as he gazed down at her. He didn't appear to move at all, but

Sharlie felt her hand being pressed closer to his side. "Well, Miss Kincaid, are you enjoying yourself this evening?"

The moment she felt his strong bicep flex beneath the covering of his charcoal jacket, Sharlie's untrained fingers twitched with the urge to pull away. Determined, she beat back the impulse.

She beamed up at him. A sexy beam.

"I certainly am. I *lo-o-ove* parties." The lie was nice and smooth. "Don't call me 'Miss Kincaid,' though. I'm just Sharlie." She gave each man's arm a warm hug. She felt almost as breezily brainless as she sounded.

Jared cleared his throat. "Well." Carefully he unwound his arm from hers and took a step back to look at her. "I found your artwork to be very...provocative, Sharlie." He inclined his head. "Just as I'm finding the artist."

"My artwork?"

"Yes." He folded his arms and watched her with a lazy look in his brown gaze.

Glen smiled. "I showed Jared a couple of the charcoal sketches you gave me. I hope you don't mind?"

"Mind?" She waved the thought away. *"Noooo."*

Mind? She felt like flinging herself at the altar of Glen's polished loafers.

Jared stared down at her. "Glen's next collection will be heavily illustrated. He thought your artwork might have possibilities, particularly since you're fond of his poetry. Or so he tells me."

Jared's attention never veered from Sharlie. Sharlie's attention never veered from Glen. Glen's attention, on the other hand, appeared lost to them both as he glanced around the room.

Sharlie didn't notice. All she saw was that his forest-green blazer looked striking with his golden hair.

She spoke intently to his profile. "I *love* his poetry. I would be *proud* to be involved."

"That couldn't be more clear."

Jared dropped his arms to his sides. His tone was low and wry. "Someone is trying to get your attention, Glen." He took Sharlie's arm in his hand when she turned her head to look at him. He continued to address Glen. "By the door," he directed. "Why don't you go meet her. I want to talk to Sharlie about her aspirations."

Before Sharlie could gather her wits, Jared took her arm and steered her toward a patio door. Glen hurried off in the opposite direction. Without thinking, Sharlie craned her neck to see whom Glen was rushing off to meet.

"You're spilling your champagne."

"What?" Sharlie blinked. There was a dark, dribbly stain on the lapel before her. The red badge of embarrassment crept up her neck and filled her face. "Oh, I'm sorry," she mumbled. "I wasn't watching..." She wiped at the stain ineffectually.

"Don't worry about it." Jared removed her hand from his suit.

"I'll clean it for you," Sharlie offered quickly, her confidence evaporating faster than the champagne. "I mean, I'll take it somewhere where they can clean it...a dry cleaners." She studied the lapel doubtfully. The stain appeared to be soaking in for a long stay. "I'm sure I know somebody who does a very good job at this sort of thing."

"Hmmm." Jared frowned as he looked up from his lapel. "If you don't mind my saying so, I think you've had all you should for one evening." He plucked the glass from her hand. "Do you usually drink so much?"

Only when I'm drinking ice water, she thought hazily. For Jared's benefit she shrugged. "We're celebrating, aren't we? This is a party."

"And you *lo-o-ove* parties."

A cool evening breeze lifted the stray strands of Sharlie's hair. What was she doing on this patio? Uncomfortably, she glanced away. She was beginning to feel more and more like her old self, and that was a very sorry state of affairs—or no affairs at all. Where had Glen disappeared to?

"I'd better get back inside." She turned, but Jared's hand on her arm stayed her steps.

"Sorry. I'm sure you know how much alcohol you can handle." He set her glass on the stone balustrade.

He was sure? *She* wasn't sure. Her pleasant giddiness was beginning to feel more like vertigo.

Jared released her arm. He regarded her carefully for a moment, then raked one hand through his thick, chestnut hair and shrugged as though he had come to a decision and, like it or not, he would follow through with it.

"I hate to be blunt on so short an acquaintance," he said with a sigh, "but stay away from Glen, Sharlie. What you're doing isn't nice, and it certainly won't be successful." He smiled a little and shook his head. "You're wasting your time with him. He's far from fickle, and no woman—even one with your persistence—is going to change his mind."

Sharlie merely stared.

"I said—"

"I heard you." She rushed to cut him off before he could say it all again. "Obviously, you've made some sort of mistake—"

"No," he corrected patiently, "you have. If I were you, I'd play it a little cooler next time, at least until you've researched your subject. For one thing, you've misjudged Glen. For another, you're trespassing on private property, Sharlie, and that's a no-no. Just so that we don't misunderstand each other, let me put it plainly—a relationship is difficult to conduct under the best of circumstances. I won't tolerate any outside interference. So find yourself another victim."

Sharlie's first thought was that life was unfair. When she'd walked into the party this evening, she'd had great hope that people would remember her as a stunning cross between Sophia Loren and Sandra Dee. Now she felt like Wally on "Leave It To Beaver."

Her next thought—and it was bolstered by the champagne—was that he had a hell of a lot of nerve for someone who wasn't making any sense.

"Wait a minute," she blinked at Jared as though her vision had just cleared. "I'm 'trespassing on private property'?" Anger and perplexity settled on her features. "Who are you, the neighborhood watch?"

Jared's eyes narrowed as he took in the sight of the small, blond, drunk woman before him. Thick strands of pretty, wavy hair were falling out of her elaborate braid. Incongruously, he decided that the hairdo didn't suit her. Too fussy. Despite the sexy pink dress and her blatant flirting, he was sure she'd be more at home in blue jeans and a ponytail.

He watched as she sucked in a deep breath, presumably to launch a verbal attack, and then tried not to reel from the effect of too much oxygen combining with too much champagne. Jared smiled.

Sharlie looked stunned for a moment as the dizziness hit her. Nonetheless, she drew herself up with an iron sense of dignity and personal empowerment. She looked Jared square in the eyes—although he suddenly appeared to have more of them than was strictly possible—and spoke slowly.

"I do not know how or why you think this is your affair—"

"My point is that I don't want it to become *your* affair."

Sharlie lost her train of thought momentarily as she focused on his words. She took another breath. She was going to have to finish this and go back inside. She was getting dizzier by the moment, and it was hot out here.

"As I shaid—said—although this is none of your business—"

"It is very much my business."

"Look. I feel secure...very secure...in saying that Glen would not appreciate your inerfere...interfrance...inferterence..." She stopped and frowned. "You shouldn't meddle. What's between Glen and me—"

"What is between Glen and you?"

"Now see here," Sharlie said angrily. "I can't interrupt if you're going to think me!"

Jared noted her flushed face and bright eyes. He folded his arms across his chest and leaned back on his heels.

"I'm sorry. I won't think you again."

"Thank you. Where was I?"

"You were about to tell me exactly what is between you and Glen."

"Oh, yes...I was? Oh, yes. Well." Glen's image came to mind, and her body responded with a warm rush of anticipation. "Well, Glen is...wonderful." She smiled. "So wonderful. We go way back in college. *Way* back." She nodded.

Jared was watching her with intent, listening eyes. Sharlie leaned forward and spoke confidentially. "I've never had much champagne before. It's very good."

"Hmmm. How close have you and Glen been recently?"

Sharlie's brow furrowed thoughtfully. She reached for the glass of champagne that was sitting on the stone balustrade. Jared's hand closed around her wrist. Gently, but very firmly, he brought her hand away from the glass and made her face him again.

"You were saying?"

She twisted her wrist free. "I don't think I was saying." Pushing primly at her bangs in an effort to clear her fuzzy vision, Sharlie blinked at Jared. "I have to go inside now." She sounded oddly staid, like a tipsy librarian.

"Sharlie," Jared's deep voice rumbled around her as firmly as his hand had held her wrist. "If there is anything between you and Glen, anything other than friendship, it's going to stop. As of right now." There was a question in his dark brown eyes.

Through her woozy haze, Sharlie recognized that it was a little exhilarating to know that somebody assumed she and Glen were actually lovers. On the other hand, this really was the nosiest man she had ever met.

"You keep butting in, but you haven't said why." She spoke slowly enough to enunciate reasonably well. "I mean, I don't know you. And what Glen does can't be any of your—" She stopped, struck by another thought.

"Oh, my God, you're gay."

Sharlie's gray eyes widened as they fastened on Jared's face. He looked as astonished as she felt. The champagne was making it remarkably easy to speak first and think later. Still, this easygoing candor was precisely what she was trying to cultivate. All her life she had run from honesty, from any type of exposure. Well, dammit, she was personally empowered, and she was going to be unrepressed if it killed her.

"I'm sorry. I didn't mean for it to come out that way. Really, I'm not at all prejudiced."

She put a hand on his arm and spoke enthusiastically. "I think it's wonderful that you're gay. I mean—" she emitted a little laugh "—what I mean is, we are what we are, so . . . so, there you are."

She smiled gently. "I do understand. Of course, I understand. I care about Glen, too. And it's not like I think I have *that* much better a chance with him just because I'm a woman. Hey, may the best person win, and I hope we'll still be friends."

She nodded up at Jared and smiled. He was staring silently, but he didn't look forbidding anymore. All things considered, this was going pretty well.

"There you are! Oops. I think I'm about to interrupt something."

Both Jared and Sharlie turned. Standing before them was
a girl who would have been perfect for Jared Wright, had
Jared Wright liked girls. She was tall, beautiful, with glossy
mink-colored hair and obviously no need for control-top
pantyhose. Her features were small and perfect, except for
her stunning amber eyes, which were large and perfect.

Jared, for his part, gave the beautiful girl one cursory
glance of acknowledgement, then turned his frowning glare
back to Sharlie. There had been not a flicker of sexual
awareness on his face when the brunette had appeared,
which confirmed Sharlie's conviction that he was long gone
on Glen.

The girl smiled. "Glen told me to come over. He's waiting for Mother and Henry to park the car." She turned her
frank gaze to Sharlie and slapped Jared lightly on the arm.
"Aren't you going to introduce us?"

"Gina, this is Sharlie. Sharlie, Gina." Jared complied
tersely, and Gina grimaced derisively.

She rolled her eyes at Sharlie. "You'll have to forgive him.
My brother has no manners."

Sharlie's attention peaked abruptly. "Brother?" She
looked at Jared. "You mean you're—"

"Related," Gina Wright admitted with mocking reluctance. "But I have much better manners." She extended a
slim, well-manicured hand. "I've really been looking forward to meeting you, Miss Kincaid."

"Call her Sharlie, she's not into formality," Jared supplied curtly. Ignoring the glance of reproof that his sister
shot at him, he curved one large hand firmly around
Sharlie's arm.

"Sharlie and I were in the middle of discussing something important when you came up, Gina. She has something she wants to explain to me, so if you'll excuse us . . ."
With very little luck, he tried to pull Sharlie swiftly through
the opened French doors.

"Oh," Gina frowned. "Well, okay, but—"

"Hey, where are you two going? I told Gina to keep you here." Glen's smoothly exuberant voice called out, and Sharlie stopped in her tracks, refusing to move while Glen approached them.

"They said they had something to discuss." Gina shrugged.

"Trying to sign her for a book deal without me?" Glen laughed. "Business waits, my friend. We've more important matters at hand."

Sharlie had eyes for only Glen. She vaguely wondered why he seemed to know all the Wrights so well, but shrugged the triviality away. She smiled at him irrepressibly.

Glen smiled back. "Jared, my man, your mother and Henry have been waylaid by old friends. But I told them to hurry, because I wasn't sure how long I could hold out." He grinned at the girl tucked neatly under his arm.

It seemed that for an eternity Sharlie had waited for this man to return her love. Now she felt like a helpless bystander as she watched him exchange looks with the lovely girl at his side. Her sense of unease was burgeoning into fear. Almost subconsciously she felt the tightening in the arm Jared draped across her shoulders. She watched desolately as Glen grinned at Gina.

"I can't wait." He looked at Sharlie. "Boy, have I got a surprise," he began.

"You sure do," Jared grumbled softly. "Glen, why don't you wait until—"

"Can't. I've been looking forward to saying this out loud. I'm getting married. Gina and I are engaged." He savored the words as he pulled the lovely brunette in for a hug. "It probably seems sudden, but I didn't want to say anything until I coerced Gina into saying yes."

"Well, it was hardly coercion," Gina Wright scoffed gently. "I've been waiting almost a year for you to ask me."

A year.

Glen shrugged, a boyish smile lighting his handsome features. "You know I'm shy. Well?" He prompted Sharlie laughingly. "Aren't you going to congratulate me?"

"Congratulations," Sharlie murmured automatically. As the numbness wore off, she began to feel a traitorous burning in her eyes and throat. "Congratulations to both of you." She heard the false exuberance in her voice, but went on, anyway. "This really did turn out to be a celebration, didn't it?"

Jared nodded smoothly. "Come on, Sharlie, let's go get the champagne to celebrate. You two stay here. We'll grab the drinks and be back for a toast." Without waiting for an argument from anybody, Jared guided Sharlie through the clusters of people filling the large room and led her out the front door and onto the stone and marble porch.

Sharlie followed along blindly this time, not caring where she was going as long as it was away from Glen.

Glen and Gina. Gina and Glen. Together. Engaged. The knowledge washed over Sharlie like a tidal wave, pounding in her ears and leaving her stunned. How long? she wondered dazedly. When? How could she not have known of it until now? She gritted her teeth to keep the questions from hurtling out. The answers didn't matter in the end.

As the night air touched her face, the tears stung her eyes, and her chest felt as if it was going to burst.

She kept her face averted. Her body felt like an earthquake was attacking it from the inside out. And her emotions—she'd be happy to pay somebody to take them off her hands for good. She closed her eyes. A little laugh that sounded like a hiccup escaped her. She felt stone-cold sober now.

A tear dripped down her cheek. It landed on the cold marble of the porch railing and was followed quickly by another. Sharlie lowered her head. A cool breeze lifted the wayward strands of her hair.

"I'm sorry, Sharlie. I would have told you myself if I'd realized earlier that you didn't know."

Jared spoke in a rich, soothing tone, but it chilled Sharlie more than the breeze. For just a moment she'd forgotten she wasn't alone. Now his presence was tangible.

Sharlie turned so that her back was all Jared saw. She felt like the emperor, parading around buck naked with a stupid smile that said, "Like my new suit?" What hadn't she said? She'd waved her feelings like a flag.

"Sharlie." Jared reached out to touch her shoulder.

His hand might as well have been a hot coal. Sharlie jerked away without turning around. Reluctantly Jared let his hand drop. He'd seen the tears slide down her cheeks; now he saw the misery in the slope of her shoulders. She looked too damn small. It occurred to him that flirting was not her customary behavior around Glen.

Still, Jared felt a surge of anger directed toward his future brother-in-law. Why hadn't Glen noticed Sharlie's feelings? He could have quelled her hopefulness long ago.

Almost against his will he recalled their earlier conversation on the balcony. He ran a hand through his brown hair and fought to stifle a grin. "Well, now we know I never would have had a chance with him."

First he saw Sharlie's back stiffen. Then she whirled, and he sobered quickly when he saw her pale, stormy face.

"I'm sorry, I—"

Sharlie didn't wait to listen. Her defenses were falling down around her, and she did the only adult thing possible under the circumstances: she ran. Ignoring the voice that again called for her to wait, she ran from the porch into the black night.

She sat in her car, in the dark, scrunched down around the stick shift where she wouldn't be seen, and cried until she felt composed. Then she drove four blocks to a café, parked her car and called a cab. She tried not to think of anything at all while the night air continued to sober her and she waited alone for the taxi to arrive.

That had been a month ago, and her life had barely moved since then. She was at a standstill, working for Esther's catering business and spending most of her time trying not to think about Glen. No matter how busy she kept herself, her mind kept wandering back to him and to the fact that at twenty-four years of age, the only hunk in her life was a thirteen-pound brisket of beef.

Sharlie shook her head. Esther was still growling about men and their flaws, and Sharlie was relieved she had told her aunt only that she had loved and lost, not that she had loved, made an idiot of herself and then lost.

What excuse had Jared made when she left the party so abruptly? Probably a snappy little improv about imminent psychosis. She had forced herself to phone Glen the next day, mumbling a few hazy words about a splitting headache, and that was when Glen had inquired—on behalf of Gina, he said—about the wedding cake. Sharlie had wanted desperately to refuse, but she hadn't known how to do it. So she said what she usually said in that situation: "Sure." At least Glen's easy manner and his unquestioning acceptance of her pitiful excuse about the headache suggested that he didn't know how she felt about him, after all. That much was a blessing. She could only hope that Jared would keep his mouth shut, if only until after the wedding.

Sharlie sighed. There was nothing to do but forget about true love and never get into this kind of situation again. She would cook and bake cakes and leave love to the people who were good at it, whoever they were. Right now all she had to do was get through this one wedding.

Of course, decorating Glen's wedding cake wasn't helping matters, Sharlie acknowledged ruefully. Somewhere in the back of that uncontrollable mind of hers was the thought that she would dazzle Glen with her culinary expertise. Throughout the ceremony his attention would be held by the loving care that had gone into the frosting.

She shook her head. He wouldn't even notice the cake until Gina stuffed it into his face for the photographer. Still, Sharlie wanted it to be perfect, so the malformed rosette would have to be fixed. She scooped more frosting into the pastry bag and bent to the task.

"Stop that!" Esther dropped the cat and reached for the pastry tube, but Sharlie was too fast for her.

"You baked it, Aunt Esther," Sharlie reminded, wrestling the bag away. She added a few quick swirls to the little frosting bud, and, satisfied with the effect, dropped the pastry tube on the counter. "You want it to look good, don't you?"

"No!" Esther insisted stubbornly. "I baked it only because you made me do it."

"I asked you to do it," Sharlie corrected, "because your cakes are always special." She scrunched her apron into a ball and pressed the wad into her aunt's arms. She sighed, bringing her hands up to rest on Aunt Esther's able, bony shoulders. "I can't explain it, Aunt Esther. I just want this cake to be something to remember."

"Huh! All right." Esther shook out the apron and gruffly lifted her cheek for Sharlie's kiss. "They'll remember it," she promised, "I guarantee it."

"Good." Sharlie gave her an affectionate peck. "Thank you."

Esther grunted. "Don't mention it." She shooed Sharlie away from the counter. "Get away from here now, and let me put these tiers together," she ordered. "You'd better start getting ready if you're going to this wedding. And try to look beautiful," Esther called out after her. "I want him to see how big a boob he's being."

Chapter Two

The calm evening breeze blowing in off the Pacific made twilight the best time of day in Southern California during the warm, warm months of spring and summer. It was the rule rather than the exception when one lived near the beach, and Sharlie had to admit that this particular April evening was as beautiful as they came.

The view from the garden of this Laguna Beach estate was a stunner. The gentle strains of a string quartet played softly in the background. Sharlie shifted slightly on the seat of her whitewashed, wooden folding chair. Beyond the wedding canopy she could see the ocean sparkling, almost shining, as the rusty-orange glow of sunset yielded gracefully to violet.

All in all, not a bad day for a wedding.

Sharlie cleared her throat and rearranged the folds of her mauve silk skirt. She had dressed well for Glen's wedding. In fact, she was proud of herself for treating this joyous occasion with the respect it deserved. She could have worn black crepe. She *would* have worn black crepe, but it was hard to find out of season.

She looked around. The seats to her right were empty, but the rest of the rows were filling up quickly now. At any moment the ceremony would begin. And her last grip on a fantasy life that would never see the light of reality would be pried loose—permanently. She smiled brightly. This was so good for her. Really. All her life she'd opted for the passive approach, which was no approach at all. She just waited for life to bring her what she wanted—like the prince arriving with the glass slipper.

She knew now that she had to change.

The string quartet moved on to the theme from *Somewhere in Time*. Sharlie shrugged. Nice choice, if you liked clichés.

She looked at the minister, a tall, gangly man with glasses, who had taken his place and was conferring with one of the groomsmen. The groomsmen were wearing beautiful dove-gray tuxedos. The man talking to the minister had his head bent forward to hear what the reverend was saying, and Sharlie wished she hadn't left her glasses in the car. She was sitting too far back to see clearly without an effort, but she thought... She inched her neck forward and squinted. He had dark hair. It could be Jared Wright.

Ducking her head behind the head of the person sitting in front of her, she peered around the woman's hair and continued to study the man at the altar. She wondered what she'd been forcing herself for a month not to think about: had he told anybody?

Somebody took the seat beside her. Sharlie shifted a bit, but continued to look toward the altar.

The tall man laughed at an anecdote the minister shared. He looked out at the guests and saw a large woman with badly teased bright red hair sitting toward the back on the groom's side. She wouldn't have drawn his attention, except that she appeared to have another head growing out of her bouffant hairdo. Blond hair, a furrowed forehead, and two squinting eyes were sticking out just above the red. When the eyes saw him turn, the half head darted behind the other woman. Frowning, the groomsman turned back to the minister.

Once he turned, Sharlie snaked forward again to see if she could make out Jared's features. If she squinted just right, and if he would turn back just a bit, she could almost identify his face in the twilight....

"Who're we looking at?" the whispered question came from her right.

Turning, she whispered back.

"Oh, I was just trying to see if I knew—"

From the seat he had taken beside her, Jared Wright smiled. His teeth were whiter than a slice of moon.

Sharlie tried valiantly to take the shocked look off her face.

"Hello," Jared said.

"Hello," she answered finally, trying to sound casually surprised to see him here, as though she'd forgotten he was the bride's brother. She studied the pink rose adorning his dove-gray lapel. "You must be a groomsman."

He glanced briefly at the boutonniere, then back up at Sharlie. She sounded bored. His lips barely moved, but his smile deepened.

"Yes, I am."

Sharlie nodded absently and moved her attention to the garden. She feigned a botanist's interest in the rose bushes.

"How have you been?" Jared ventured.

The question seemed innocuous, but Jared had lowered his voice to ask it, and Sharlie sensed that if she looked at him, he'd have that sensitive-male look on his face. She didn't look at him.

"I've been fine," she trilled airily. "Busy."

"Glen said you're a caterer. Busy time of year?"

"Oh, yes," she nodded, moving her gaze to the snap-dragon bed. Her lips tightened grimly. "A lot of weddings."

He leaned a bit closer. Sharlie could smell his after-shave. Somehow it blended beautifully with the sea air and the rose bushes. She stared at the red beehive of the woman in front of her.

Jared watched her unblinking profile. "Sharlie, I motion for a truce. You did say you hoped we'd be friends."

Jared knew it was dirty pool to remind her of what she'd said to him at the party, but, hell, it worked. Her whole face tightened, and she blinked once.

"That was when I thought you were gay."

He laughed, the carefree laugh, Sharlie thought, of a man who had not made a fool of himself.

"Are you going to be okay tonight?" he asked her.

Sharlie faced him. He looked sincere; there was nothing snide, no baiting in the question. She felt tears threaten at the back of her eyes. She shrugged nonchalantly to belie her feelings.

"Oh, yes," she tossed off dryly, turning to face front again. "Actually, I'm relieved. I found out Glen *is* gay."

Jared laughed. He sounded satisfied when he spoke. "I guess you'll be fine."

He stood and stared down at her until her gaze rose involuntarily to his. She saw the humor in his dark eyes.

"Save a dance for me at the reception."

In a pig's eye, would have been too rude to say, so Sharlie stayed ambiguously silent. She pretended not to watch Jared walk up the aisle to take his place near the minister. Then her attention was caught and held by Glen, who walked in grinning, shook Jared's hand and greeted the minister. He turned with an even bigger grin to watch the bridal party begin their nervous walk down the aisle.

Sharlie willed herself not to stare. At anyone. She was going to get out of here right after the ceremony. It would be cruel and inhumane to make herself stay for the reception. She would plead a headache or emergency root canal later, but she would not be seen sobbing at this reception.

The wedding march began, and the guests stood. Smiles popped up on the faces turned toward the bride. Sharlie looked at Glen. Her eyes adjusted to the light and the distance enough for her to see that he was watching his bride with more love and tenderness than Sharlie had ever seen on a face. She lost her concentration for the rest of the ceremony. She stood when the other guests stood, joined in the group prayer and smiled when the vows were spoken.

Then it was over. The bride and groom kissed. Sharlie closed her eyes. She shouldn't have to watch this; it would be bad enough imagining it for the next twelve years. She rubbed the bridge of her nose as if she were merely resting her vision. When she looked up again, Jared was watching her. She started to plaster a bright, empty smile on her face, but her lips would not cooperate. What difference did it make? They were married, and she was miserable. When you were twenty-four and your only prospect for a hot date was your cat, you didn't owe anybody any explanations.

Glen and Gina were coming down the aisle. Sharlie was sitting near the end of the row; how hard could it be to trip them?

As they passed, Glen never took his eyes off his wife. Sharlie sat with her hands clutching her purse, ready to bolt.

The happy couple was followed by Jared and the maid of honor. Sharlie kept her head averted, but she heard the voice of his partner as they passed. The pretty redhead was laughing.

"You're next, Jared, darling."

Jared darling mumbled something low in reply, and the pair strolled off, followed by the rest of the bridal party.

As the last couple disappeared to a side garden for pictures, Sharlie stood and moved with the flow of traffic heading toward the champagne and hors d'oeuvres inside the house. She ignored the baby brie in puff pastry, shuddered at the champagne and hastened past her cake without a glance. Her heels clicked on the marble floor. She walked out of the house, found her car and drove home under a sky that had surrendered to the night.

And Sharlie surrendered to the tears that, temporarily at least, seemed to fill the empty place inside of her.

The tiny catering shop was closed when she arrived in Corona del Mar. Aunt Esther had apparently gone home to her own cottage in Laguna Beach, so Sharlie let herself in through the back, shuffling up the darkened staircase to her apartment. Lotty greeted her at the door and took a flying leap at Sharlie's feet from the back of a green tweed easy chair. The little cat swatted a note that was lying on the rug near the door. Sharlie bent down to retrieve the paper before it was shredded.

"Hello, cat." She gave the furry body a cuddle and unfolded the note. It was from Esther.

Your cat ate my braised kidneys. Tomorrow's birthday brunch is now ruined. I withheld her evening ice cream as punishment.

Love, Your Aunt

"Darn it, Lotty!" Sharlie moaned, depositing the cat on the couch and dropping down next to her. "Rotten cat," she scolded.

Lotty sprang off the couch and crouched guiltily under the coffee table. Sharlie's eyes dropped to the postscript.

P.S. I did what I had to do. Call me if you are very angry with me.

Sharlie frowned. Talk about disciplining the cat? She re-

read the P.S. Strange. Usually Esther had few qualms about chasing Lotty around the store with a frying pan poised in swatting position above the cat's head.

"And you deserve it, too," Sharlie snapped, waving the note at her troublesome feline. "Now I've got to stay up all night making braised kidneys for twenty, and it's your fault! Braised kidneys," Sharlie groaned, her voice beginning to quiver. "I hate braising kidneys. I don't even like to look at them."

She crumpled the note and tossed it at the unconcerned cat. "This is a rotten night. A rotten, rotten, horrible night."

It had been stupid to think she could worship a man secretly for years and blindly assume that he was returning the favor. But crying because your heart was breaking over a man who never had noticed your existence, anyway—except as the buddy you had been to him—that really took the cake.

However, if in almost twenty-five years no man had ever found you of romantic interest, then you were entitled to cry your eyeballs out. Sharlie flung an arm over her eyes and sat there, glad there was only Lotty to watch her make a fool of herself.

And so, when finally she lifted her arm from her eyes, the digital clock had already clicked to eight twenty-five. She had been sitting here long enough to grow barnacles. It was time to move, she told herself firmly, time to go braise kidneys.

Hauling herself off the couch and over to the tiny bathroom, Sharlie flicked on the light and nearly gasped at the reflection in the mirror. The hair she had styled so carefully for the wedding was a disaster. Heavy blond waves fell everywhere but in the braid she had labored so long to create. Her waterproof mascara was streaked halfway down her cheeks, and her eyes were so red and swollen she looked like a rodent.

"That's what crybabies get," she told the unhappy reflection mercilessly.

She washed the makeup off her face and pulled the pins out of her hair, letting the stubborn curls fall where they would. Peering into the mirror, she sighed. She still looked like a field rat; her eyes were so puffy, they appeared half-closed. Admitting defeat, Sharlie changed into a sweatshirt and a pair of jeans and headed downstairs. One need not look one's best for an evening rendezvous with five pounds of kidneys.

Lotty bounded on down ahead of her, and Sharlie clung on to the narrow banister, trying not to trip over the cat in the dark. In the kitchen she threw on the lights and padded over to a huge freezer unit that was built into the wall.

"Do not tell Aunt Esther I'm doing this," she warned as she pulled a quart container of Esther's homemade coconut chocolate-bar ice cream out of the freezer. Grabbing a spoon and a bowl from one of the cupboards, Sharlie scooped a generous portion of the ice cream into the dish and took it to a counter away from her work area.

"Eat this," she told a more-than-willing Lotty, "and don't even think about the kidneys." As Sharlie watched the cat greedily stick her face into the bowl, she marveled at the vast quantities and varieties of food that went into that tiny body.

"This catering job's okay with you, huh, pigface?" She smiled as a purr rumbled inside the blissful animal. "So that's all it takes, hmm?" she mused. "A little ice cream, and the world looks all right to you."

Thoughtful, Sharlie dipped the spoon into the quart tub. Ice cream was a nice food, cool and smooth and comforting. All white food was comforting. Cream of Wheat, mashed potatoes, whipped cream—they were all white, and they were all comforting.

She put the spoon in her mouth. The ice cream slid over her tongue like silk. Rich, sweet and creamy. Ice-cream heaven. She plunged the spoon back into the container and dug out a huge, dark chunk of chocolate. She popped it into her mouth and sent the spoon back for more.

Scoop, lift, swallow; scoop, lift, swallow. The process continued until Sharlie had to lean over the counter to rest. Each mouthful was a little more numbing than the last. Her jeans were beginning to pinch like crazy, but her emotions were growing considerably duller.

Gazing into the liquid swirls of ice cream, Sharlie thought that the old adage about a spoonful of sugar really was true; Mary Poppins knew her stuff. If there was a universal panacea, it was sugar.

She stirred the ice cream lazily, lifting the spoon and letting the soupy liquid dribble back into the container. Chunks of chocolate bobbed and then sank in a coconut sea. Maybe one more teensy taste; then she would be numbed completely, totally rid of all emotion as she gave in completely to her food stupor.

Up came the spoon, dripping and sticky. A piece of chocolate was marooned in the center, waiting to be claimed. Sharlie opened her mouth. Just one more bite—

"Open the door, dammit!"

The voice seemed to come from nowhere, booming into the silence of the night, and Sharlie jumped. The spoon went flying as she whirled to locate the disembodied voice.

"Wh-who—" she stuttered. "Wh-where—" Her heart was pounding a mile a minute.

"I know you're in there. You open this door or so help me, Sharlie, I'll open it myself."

'Sharlie'? Whoever this madman pounding on her door was, he knew her name. The door rattled to punctuate his threat, and Sharlie took a timid step toward it. The voice had startled her so, her heart still felt like it was going to hammer right out of her chest. She took a steadying breath to calm the pounding and walked to the door. Pushing aside the long, melon-colored shade that covered the glass, she peered out into the night.

The beam of the street lamp poured down onto the sidewalk, highlighting the dark, ruffled hair of the man beyond the glass. His topaz eyes sparkled in the night.

"What are you doing here?" Sharlie stared in befuddled wonder at Jared Wright.

"Open the door." The words seethed with impatience.

Running a hand through her hair—and only then realizing that the hand was sticky with ice cream—Sharlie unbolted the door and inched it open.

"We're closed for the eve—" she began, but Jared put a firm hand on the door and pushed it open, brushing by Sharlie without apology.

She turned to glare at him, but it was wasted. The room had his full attention for the moment, and he was staring at the mess in fascination.

Ice cream seemed to be everywhere. It was melted in little puddles on the counter and splattered over the floor where the spoon had landed. Sharlie's face flushed as she looked at the condemning evidence of her food orgy. Self-consciously, she moved to the sink in order to wash the sticky evidence off her hands. When she turned back to Jared, he was watching her with the same disapproving grimace he gave the messy floor.

Sharlie supposed she should speak first, but there was a gleam of mockery on his handsome face, and despite her desire to remain unruffled, she felt too uncomfortable to speak.

Jared filled the silence. "We missed you at the reception, Sharlie."

She shrugged. "I couldn't make it. I had an appointment."

"With whom? The Good Humor Man?"

"My cat was hungry," she grumbled defensively.

"He likes ice cream?"

"She," Sharlie corrected tersely. "Yes, she does."

"Interesting cat." A half smile curved Jared's mouth.

He wandered to the center island and peered unabashedly into the container of ice cream.

Sharlie tugged her sweatshirt down.

Jared leaned against the counter, his hands resting on hips still covered by gray tuxedo trousers. "Your cat has quite a sweet tooth. Good thing you didn't feed her any of the wedding cake, isn't it?"

Sharlie looked at him blankly. "Why would I feed my cat wedding cake?"

Jared's eyes narrowed. "Why indeed? Certainly no one with a sweet tooth would appreciate your cake, would they?"

"What are you talking about?" Now Sharlie was becoming annoyed.

Straightening away from the counter, Jared took a menacing step toward her. "Don't play games with me, Sharlie. Have the guts to admit what you did. Somehow I'd hoped for that much from you. I want to know why you did it."

Sharlie stared at him open-mouthed. "I'd like to know what you're talking about, but we can't have everything."

She turned to the door, ready to open it and show him out, but he grabbed her arm and turned her back to face him.

"Oh, no." He smiled grimly. "Neither of us is going anywhere until you tell me why you tried to ruin a young girl's wedding. What did you hope to gain?" He let go of her arm, but his candid eyes held her.

"You sat at that wedding like you were running a gauntlet. I thought it was tough on you, but given the circumstances, you have quite a poker face." He shook his head, anger pressing into his features and into the voice he was trying to control. "But why did you leave before the big finish?" He moved closer to her. "Did your courage run out on you? Or did your sanity suddenly return?"

Sharlie was backed against the door, and the bells on the knob jingled as she bumped them. The tinkling punctuated his words like the foreshadowing music of a B movie.

"Was there something wrong with the cake?"

Blatant disgust filled his strong body until every muscle seemed to tense with it. One large hand came up to rest on the wall on either side of Sharlie's head, and he leaned toward her.

Sharlie blinked behind her glasses. His face was so close to hers, she could see the dark shadow of stubble forming along the lean jaw. Even the warm, musky scent of the after-shave he had used that morning was discernible, and the sight of dark hairs curling beneath the opening of his shirt collar uncomfortably reminded Sharlie that she had rarely stood this close to a man, particularly one who was ready to breathe fire.

Feeling distinctly threatened, she sought to end this situation as quickly as possible. "I'm sorry if you felt there was something wrong with the cake. If you want a refund, you can have it. Frankly, I'm sure you're exaggerating, but—"

"Exaggerating? Glen wouldn't think so," he told her, obviously hoping to draw a reaction. "Gina pushed a piece into his mouth and he nearly choked on it."

"Maybe she pushed it in too far."

"Don't be flip," Jared warned. "We all tasted it. We cut into every tier. Jalepeños in one layer, what I assume was chili powder in the next. I don't even want to know what you added to the anniversary cake. You did your work very thoroughly."

Sharlie regarded him stonily. She was suddenly struck with the sick thought that he might be telling the truth. And if it was the truth...

"You could actually taste jalepeños? Sometimes we use green candied cherries, and they look like—" She didn't bother to finish. The answer was clear from the expression on his face. The postscript to Esther's note about the braised kidneys was infused with new meaning. *I did what I had to.*

Oh, Aunt Esther, of all the things to have done! Her highly professional, tiny, gray-haired aunt had sabotaged an entire four-tiered wedding cake. Glen must have been furious, must still be furious. Well, at least she didn't have to worry about the intricacy of maintaining a friendship with him now that he was married: after this disaster, he would never want to speak with her again. In fact, she thought, he probably sent Jared here to yell at her because he didn't want to wait until after the honeymoon to see the job done.

"Did Glen tell you to come here?"

Her question was met by a black scowl. "You should have worried about what Glen would say before you got creative," he told her, adding, "not that what he thinks or feels or does has anything whatsoever to do with you anymore, Sharlie. Unfortunately my naive brother-in-law thinks this whole mess was a perfectly innocent mistake. Since we both know better, I'm going to issue a little warning. Stay away from my sister's husband. One move toward him or a single repeat of an episode like today's, and I'll have this shop closed inside of a week."

Jared stared down at her, expecting a retort. When none came, he nodded sharply. "Fine, then we understand each other."

He brought his arms down and leaned away from Sharlie several inches before reaching around behind her to grasp the doorknob.

Maintaining her silence, Sharlie slid away from the door. She kept her eyes on him as he started to leave, surprised when he stopped inside the door to turn and regard her again.

His expression was enigmatic, his voice more dulcet than she had yet heard it. "For everyone's sake, I hope you can forget him."

He looked at her a moment longer, and Sharlie expected him to move away, but he surprised her once more by leaning into her as he stared. Reflexively her head inched back. Jared's expression seemed to be changing softly, subtly, as his head came nearer. But his face was still unreadable. The closer he came, the more nonchalant Sharlie struggled to feel. It was a losing battle.

Jared paused with barely a breath of space between their faces, and she stood mesmerized as he brought one handsomely manicured finger up to touch the corner of her mouth. After a moment, his finger fell away, a slight curve claimed his lips, and his mouth was on hers with a whisper-smooth firmness. The tip of his tongue brushed the corner of her mouth that his finger had grazed. He brought his head away, and his tongue dabbed at his own lips almost experimentally.

He looked at her with a question, one eyebrow raised. "Coconut?" He nodded lightly, pointed to her mouth, and advised, "Next time your cat has a sweet tooth, better remind her to wipe off the evidence."

He nodded and walked through the door, closing it behind him with a soft click.

Sharlie waited a few moments. When she was sure he had driven away, she walked to the door and locked it. Leaning against the door, she sighed, but there was no relaxation to be found, no tension released, and the sigh turned into a groan. She had the overwhelming urge to pound her forehead against the door frame. What next? What more humiliation could she suffer?

No, don't ask, she told herself firmly, you'll surely get an answer. Spying the phone, she took three angry strides and reached for the pink receiver, ready to call Esther and ask the woman what had possessed her to risk both her own professional reputation and Sharlie's last shred of dignity in order to pull this crazy stunt. Four digits into the phone number, however, Sharlie replaced the receiver.

It wouldn't do any good at all to yell at her aunt. Esther didn't give a fig about incidentals like professional reputation and personal dignity when revenge was at stake.

Sharlie shook her head miserably. All she could do now was let sleeping dogs lie. And she would do her human best to avoid Glen. She could never tell him the truth about who ruined the cake—or why; it would be too embarrassing for her and too damaging to her aunt's shop. So Glen would go on believing she was malicious. Under the circumstances, it was hard to decide which was worse.

Knowing she was too tired, too full of ice cream and too depressed to clean up, and feeling no compunction about leaving a sticky mess downstairs while she went upstairs, Sharlie decided she would go to bed now and get up early in the morning to clean the kitchen and braise the kidneys. Between now and dawn she would try to sleep and avoid all contact with reality.

Shaking her head at the inscrutability of the fates—and her aunt Esther—Sharlie started up the stairs. On the third step, her foot came down on something soft, and a loud meow echoed in the darkened hallway. Lotty jumped up and ran between Sharlie's legs to get away. Sharlie tripped up the next step, slamming her right foot into the stair.

"Owwwww!" She grabbed the railing and stumbled to sit on the stairs. She held her throbbing foot and moaned, "Lotty!"

Tears burned in her eyes as she rocked back and forth against the pain centering on her big toe.

It was the perfect capper to a lousy evening.

Chapter Three

"Please, please make him stop pacing, Henry. I'm already seasick, and we haven't even boarded the ship." Julia Wright Burns placed one hand to her stomach and laid the other on the knee of her new husband.

Henry Burns patted his wife's hand soothingly. He looked up at his stepson in mute appeal.

Jared stopped pacing in deference to his mother, but he absolutely, flatly refused to quit scowling. A man in his position was entitled to grimace.

"Mother," he began patiently, "what I don't understand is how you could wait until now to tell me this."

"Then you weren't listening." Julia Wright patted her short, dark hair and gave a fluttery wave of her hand before allowing it to fall gracefully back to her lap. "We thought your sister and Glen might enjoy running the inn while we are in Europe. However, Glen has taken a summer school position down south." A native of Northern California, Julia always referred to the southern portion of her home state as though it were Dixie.

Jared stood before his mother in the large wood and plaid library of her bed and breakfast inn, The Fruit of the Vine. He was determined to be calm.

"Mother, you're going to have to hire someone to run the inn for you this summer."

"No-o-o," she said, and the disappointment on her face was almost admonishing. "This is a family-run inn. It says so in all the brochures. Besides, Mrs. Manzer does the difficult work. The most you would have to do is make sure the checks don't bounce. And anyway, you need to get away from the office. You said so yourself. You were talking about a vacation."

"I was talking about four days in Seattle."

Julia's sharp brows lowered. "Precisely my point. Four days isn't a vacation; it's a field trip!" She turned to her husband with a look of girlish appeal. "Henry, dear, would you get me an iced tea? There's a pitcher in the refrigerator. Oh, and stir a little honey into the whole batch," she added as Henry dutifully rose and went to the door. "Honey is so good with hibiscus tea, as long as you don't use clover honey. I think I have some orange blossom in the little pot your sister brought me from England. Use the orange blossom, Henry. My throat is simply parched from listening to Jared."

Henry smiled at his bride and left without a word.

Julia stayed silent a moment, calmly watching her son. When she spoke, her voice was reflective and quietly strong.

"I wasn't fair to you. When your father left—"

Jared's wince was just perceptible before he turned away. He hated any mention of the father who had left without word and without ever returning.

"When your father left," Julia repeated, "I let myself lean on you."

"I wanted to—" Jared began.

"You were only fifteen. You started taking care of your sister and of me almost twenty years ago and you've never stopped. I had hoped when I married Henry, and then when Gina married…'' She sighed. ''I should have seen to it that you had an irresponsible phase.''

Jared turned back to his mother with a gentle grin that was almost boyish. ''And you want me to have one now, with your inn?''

Julia's brown eyes, a prototype of her son's, twinkled. ''Smart one. I want you to take some time to think about your life.''

''Have I been doing so badly?''

''You're a clever, hard-working man, and I'm as proud as a mother can be of all you've accomplished.'' Julia had never had a moment's worry about her son's career.

Jared had started his own publishing company at an impossibly young age. He'd cajoled and he'd pushed and he'd confronted when he'd had to, in order to find the backing that would give birth to a small press, an independent publishing house that would produce eclectic works by new artists. No one had believed the venture would be a commercial success, but no one knew her son, Julia thought with pleasure. Brilliant promotion, careful marketing and the smarts to surround himself with intelligent people went a long, long way.

Now Julia was simply asking that a few of those intelligent people take over for a piddling four months. She could hire somebody to oversee the management of the inn; she didn't need Jared for that. But she did need to give something to her son. She needed to give him what he'd been denied all those years ago: freedom, the chance to view his life unencumbered, the chance to see. He'd lost that when his father had left and he had tried so valiantly and so persistently to make up for the loss. If she was right, Jared would find that something was missing.

Julia adjusted a charm bracelet that tinkled on her wrist. 'You wouldn't have to stay here every day for four months, you know. San Francisco isn't that far. You could go into your office from time to time. You could bring your work back here—occasionally," she warned him.

"Mom, you do all the cooking here. I can't cook."

"Hire someone."

"I have one month until the start of the season. Are you going to give me any suggestions about who I should hire?"

Julia shrugged. "What about that little girl who did your sister's wedding cake?"

"Are you crazy?!"

Wincing, Julia hunched her shoulders protectively toward her ears. "Don't shout, sweetheart. Where *is* Henry?" Her son looked as if he was about to pace again. Julia frowned. "You said she wasn't responsible for the cake."

"I said I *thought* she wasn't responsible." Jared paused and shook his head. He hadn't told his mother or anyone else about Sharlie's infatuation. It was Glen who told them that in all likelihood Sharlie had only decorated the cake. "Even if she wasn't responsible, that leaves her aunt, which still means lunacy runs in the family."

Julia laughed. "The icing was excellent. I like fondant."

Jared stared at his mother in bald disbelief.

"Oh, of course I was upset, at first. Really, Jared, lighten up! How many cakes do you remember eating at weddings? No one will ever forget your sister's cake. You know, sometimes I think your sister and I got all the humor in the family. Where's your sense of the absurd?"

It was back in Corona del Mar with a bespectacled, curly-headed caterer he hadn't been able to get out of his mind for two weeks. But even if the idea was intriguing—

"She works alone with her aunt," he told his mother. "I doubt she would leave. Apparently her aunt is over eighty."

"Her aunt is only seventy-nine. Glen is horrible with numbers. Do you know he thought *I* was in my sixties?" Julia, who would turn sixty this summer on the Côte d'Azur, pursed her lips testily.

"How do you know how old her aunt is?"

"I called her myself yesterday. And I think you'll find her very amenable to the idea of her niece working here for a few months. Glen tells me Charlene is a lovely girl."

" 'Charlene'?"

"Oh, for heaven's sake, Jared," Julia snapped. "You stared at the girl through the whole wedding ceremony. I'm surprised your sister didn't slap you. Didn't you even get her name? Really, I need that tea!"

"I got her name," Jared murmured, turning again from his mother to look out the window—and to hide the smile that was tugging insistently at his lips. If he was going to work with Sharlie all summer, they would need to install a boxing ring on the patio.

"Does she want to work here?" he asked his mother.

"Her aunt hasn't mentioned it to her yet. You'll have to finalize everything, dear. Esther says it would be better if we approach her niece discreetly, without saying immediately that we're related to Glen. Apparently, Charlene doesn't like handouts." Julia smiled approvingly. "I did mention to Esther that you and Charlene had already met, and that I was certain you would see to it that she feels comfortable here."

Julia found no reason to add that Esther was far more interested in Jared than she was in the salary. A woman after Julia's own heart.

In the contest of wills between Jared's logic and his desire, desire was winning. He did need a vacation, and it would be stimulating, to say the least, to have Sharlie around all summer. Not that it wouldn't also be good for Sharlie. Glen and Gina would be moving to Orange County after their honeymoon. There was a distinct advantage to having Sharlie a few hundred miles away from them. Sharlie was too easily hurt. The distance and the time would give her a chance to heal, to get over her infatuation with Glen. Jared wanted that for her. After all, like it or not he was already involved.

Julia saw the furrow on Jared's brow and knew instantly that her only son was being logical. She signed. His next words failed to surprise her.

"All right, I'll send an offer down. It might work out. It would be good practical experience for Sharlie. And I'll be here to make sure things run smoothly." He nodded, satisfied.

"Yes, dear, I'm sure you'll consider all the practicalities. Where *is* Henry?! Oh. You know, I think I used all the orange blossom honey. He's probably still searching for it. So literal."

Julia rose gracefully from the sofa and walked to the door. "Oh, and dear," she said, pausing with her hand on the knob, "try not to let things run *too* smoothly this summer, hmm?"

The sky was clear, and the beach weather beckoned. Sharlie ignored the call as she finished her work on twenty-two chocolate cupcakes that had to be decorated to look like caps and tassels for a graduation party. Frowning over the challenge of creating edible mortarboards, Sharlie didn't bother to look up when the door jingled to herald Aunt Esther's entrance with the morning mail.

"Anything for me?"

"Maybe," her aunt replied, slitting envelopes at random without identifying the addressee. "How's your foot?"

"Fine." The toe she'd sprained on the stairs three weeks ago was finally on the mend.

Sharlie hadn't told her aunt about Jared Wright's visit and her aunt hadn't asked about the spicy cake. They both pretended to forget about the entire episode. Or rather Sharlie pretended. Knowing Esther, she really had dismissed the incident from her mind by now.

"You got a three-dollar rebate on that blow dryer you bought. Fry your hair with that thing," Esther announced, holding out a check for Sharlie's examination. "If you ask me, you ought to put the money toward a good haircut. Something to bring out the curl. and you could use new makeup, too. I don't like what you have on.''

"I'm not wearing any.''

"Well, there you go then.''

Sharlie swallowed a sigh and focused on the cupcakes. Esther continued the scrutiny.

"You're too fair to go without makeup. Get something to bring out your eyes. And buy something pretty to wear instead of those jeans all the time.''

"You want me to wear silk to frost a cupcake?''

"No, I want you to dress nicely and start going out places! You're a pretty girl. Buy a nice sundress.''

"Sure," Sharlie scoffed with a laugh. "With my skin, I'd look like a light bulb with freckles in a sundress.''

"No, you won't. You can get a pretty pastel color. And shoes to match.''

"You want me to do all this on a three-dollar rebate?''

"I'll give you an advance on your next check. The department stores on Fashion Island are having a sale—''

"I'll wait until my next paycheck. Is there any other mail for me?'' Sharlie tried to close the issue.

"I don't know, and if you wait for your next paycheck, the sale might be over.''

"I'll go take a look after work," Sharlie relented with a groan.

"Today?'' her aunt prodded.

"Yes, all right, today!'' Sharlie gave in, exasperated. She knew her looks could use a lift, but she hadn't realized the situation was so desperate. Maybe she would lose five pounds and then go shopping. "Any other mail?''

"I don't know. You look." Esther tossed the remaining envelopes on the counter, bored now with the mail. "What are you going to do about those mortarboards?'' she asked, frowning at the cupcake Sharlie was working on.

"I don't know." Sharlie wiped chocolatey fingers on her apron and reached for the envelopes. "I thought I'd use thin slabs of that bittersweet chocolate you bought and attach them to the rest of the cupcake with frosting. Then I'll decorate the chocolate."

"Hmph. Sounds like it's going to cost me a fortune."

"Well, what did you charge per cupcake?"

"A fortune," her aunt admitted grudgingly, "but that's beside the point. I have to turn a profit."

"You will," Sharlie assured her absently, examining an envelope with a curious return address. "Did you send for information from a place called," she peered at the name, "The Fruit of the Vine Inn in Carmel, California?"

Esther shook her head. "Never heard of it," she lied. "Maybe they're doing publicity mailings."

"I don't think so. It's addressed to you personally."

"Open it up and see what they want," Esther dismissed with a wave of her hand. Sharlie ripped open the envelope. As she examined the letter and accompanying materials, her gray eyes widened, and a look of pure amazement filled her face.

Esther licked a dab of frosting off her finger. "What do they want?"

"They want us!" Sharlie laughed. "It says they need a chef for their season starting in late June and that we were recommended to them—get this—'with the highest praise,'" she quoted. "They want us to send someone from the shop to the inn." Sharlie laughed in amazement. "I can't believe it."

"What do you mean, you can't believe it?" Esther demanded indignantly. "We're excellent. We should be recommended."

Sharlie grinned at her aunt's immodesty. "But this place has to be over three hundred miles away."

"I've heard of Le Cordon Bleu and they're farther than that. Let me see that letter." She plucked the paper from

Sharlie's fingers, her sharp eyes traveling over the contents quickly, as she walked to the phone.

Sharlie frowned. "What are you doing?"

"It says to call. I'm calling."

Sharlie listened attentively as Esther spoke with the Mrs. Manzer who had signed the letter. Rather than thanking the woman for the offer and then turning it down as Sharlie had expected her to, Esther asked pertinent questions about the demands of the job. Her aunt questioned Mrs. Manzer about the type of traveler the inn attracted this time of year, and then finally, to Sharlie's utter consternation, Esther began to haggle over the salary. When she seemed content with whatever agreement had been reached, she casually replaced the receiver and turned back to her niece. "She's going to speak with the owner of the inn about our salary demands and then call us back. That'll give us some time to mull it over."

"Mull what over? We can't close the shop for a whole summer to work at somebody's inn."

"We don't have to close the shop. That would defeat the purpose."

Sharlie shook her head. "What is the purpose?"

Esther reached across the counter to snatch a piece of chocolate. She smiled. "The purpose," she said, nibbling at a corner of the square, "is to beef up our prestige. When you come back," *if* you come back, she amended mentally, "we can advertise that we have the chef from an exclusive, no, a *famous* Northern California inn. People love that."

"Is this place that well-known?" Sharlie asked, eyes wide.

Esther shrugged. "Never heard of it. But who will know? Plus, this inn isn't that far from San Francisco. You can make a couple of trips to restaurants there and bring back a few ideas." Her eyes narrowed as they assessed the blond hair that hung in heavy waves to Sharlie's shoulders. Bangs were the only concession to style. "You can get a good haircut while you're there, too. Go to Neiman Marcus on

Geary Street. As I recall, they have a wonderful beauty salon, and you can get a few outfits afterward."

"What is wrong with my hair?" Sharlie demanded, her
hand coming up to smooth the bangs that curled no matter
how long she blew them dry.

"Don't get me started," her aunt warned bluntly. "It's a
cute style, but you're too old for cute. And I think I'd like
you blonder."

Sharlie made a face. "I'm not going to dye my hair." Esther started to argue, but Sharlie interrupted. "It doesn't
matter, anyway, because no one is going to San Francisco."

"Oh yes," Esther nodded. "I think you should go."

Sharlie stared at her aunt, dumbfounded. "We just got
the letter ten minutes ago, and already your mind is made
up," she accused. "You can't just decide things like this in
ten seconds, Aunt Esther. If I go, how are you going to keep
up with all of your clients? There's plenty to do here during
the summer with just the two of us, you know."

"I'm not an old lady yet, Charlene Kincaid!" Esther
leaned across the counter toward Sharlie, her small face as
serious and as intent as Sharlie had ever seen it. "But you
know what? You are. You act like an old woman. You're so
afraid to shake yourself up a little. Take a risk, or you'll be
old way before I am."

Esther pursed her lips to keep from saying more, and
stalked into the kitchen. A moment later, Sharlie heard the
hiss and crackle of meat hitting a fry pan.

She gazed out the window at the lazy mid-morning traffic along their stretch of the Pacific Coast Highway. Esther
was right. She did hate to shake herself up. No matter how
frustrated she felt, she never seemed to be able to take the
steps necessary to dispel the feeling.

There was a traffic light not far from the shop, and the
sound of a motorist revving his car's engine while he waited
for the green made the cars seem like horses at the starting
gate. Everyone was in such a hurry to go somewhere. Sharlie

shook her head. She had trouble just finding somewhere to go. Her glance flickered to the letter lying open on the counter. Maybe. She picked up the letter and turned it over in her hands and in her mind as she carried it into the kitchen.

Two weeks later, Sharlie was in her lemon-yellow Volvo, circa 1968, heading up Interstate 101 to the Fruit of the Vine Inn. Lotty was snoozing on the seat beside her. Esther had seen several advantages to Sharlie's accepting the temporary position at the inn, not the least of which was the golden opportunity to take a vacation of her own from her niece's cat.

Her aunt's friend Beverly was looking forward with great relish to filling in at the shop while Sharlie was away, and Esther seemed to be looking forward to having her there. Esther's greatest pleasure, however, derived from her unshakable belief that working at the inn would be the experience of a lifetime for Sharlie. Sharlie felt like she was being sent to summer camp.

"You'll meet people, you'll get your hair done. Mrs. Manzer told me that they get quite a few writers at that inn," her aunt had told her suggestively.

Four hours and one shared meatloaf sandwich later, Sharlie and Lotty pulled into the cobbled driveway of the Fruit of the Vine Inn. The inn looked friendly, even at night. It was all wood and stone and clinging ivy vines, and Sharlie was sure that daylight would reveal a loveliness that could only be hinted at in the evening light.

Lotty had been sleeping on Sharlie's lap for the last hour, but she was awake and stretching now. Sharlie scratched behind the oversized ears, then scooped the cat up to carry her to the door. Her quiet knocking was answered almost immediately by a pretty auburn-haired woman whose welcoming smile was framed by dimples.

"You must be Sharlie! I'm Mrs. Manzer. Come in, come in. I spoke with your aunt over the phone." Mrs. Manzer's cheerful face and demeanor made Sharlie feel immediately at home, and she felt grateful already that this woman was going to be her employer. The older woman turned warm brown eyes to Sharlie and started to say something, when all at once her smile dropped.

"Is that a cat?" she asked, her brows drawing into a frown.

Sharlie looked at the animal squirming in her arms. Puzzled, she nodded. "Is that going to be a problem?"

No-o-o, perhaps not. No one mentioned anything about a cat, though.

Aunt Esther! Sharlie fumed silently. Outwardly she smiled brightly. "I'm sorry, I was under the impression that my aunt had discussed this with you." *They're delighted to have her,* were Esther's exact words. "I'm very sorry." Sharlie apologized, the words sounding woefully lame and inadequate.

"Oh, no, that's all right. I have explicit orders that you're to be as comfortable as possible—" her brown eyes twinkled "—so I'm sure it's all right that you brought your little cat. I shouldn't have mentioned it."

"Orders?" Sharlie questioned, utterly confused. "But I thought you were the owner."

"Me?" Mrs. Manzer laughed. "No. I'm the housekeeper. The head housekeeper. And the secretary when need be. Why don't I show you your room now? You had a long drive, you poor little thing. Are you hungry?"

Sharlie replied that she was fine and meekly followed Mrs. Manzer up the stairs.

"This is your room. I hope everything is the way you like it. We can meet downstairs in the kitchen tomorrow morning, and I'll give you a tour and tell you a little more about the job."

After ensuring that her new chef was comfortable, Mrs. Manzer bustled out, leaving Sharlie to gaze in pleasure at her temporary home.

It was decorated in brown and beige with accents of rose. The furniture was country antique, the bed a beautiful four-poster that made Sharlie want to crawl into it right away. It was all so lovely, she felt like she was on vacation. It was a romantic setting, and suddenly Sharlie felt very lucky indeed. A new setting could do a lot for the spirit. Maybe her spirit would feel free here, and daring. After all, as Aunt Esther said, a lot of male writers stayed here.

Mulling that thought over, Sharlie stretched out on the soft, quilted comforter and yawned happily. Better not get too comfortable, she warned herself drowsily, you still have to bring everything in from the car. On that note she drifted off into a sweet dream of country inns and petal-colored cakes, a simple world in which charming men sampled her baking and immediately fell in love.

The aroma of wine sauce and fresh herbs filled the homey kitchen the following evening, signaling anyone within smelling distance that dinner was about to be served. Sharlie pulled a baking pan of hot poppyseed rolls from the oven and placed it carefully on the counter. She put the finishing touches on a colorful salad and popped it into the refrigerator to chill, then poured herself an iced tea and surveyed the bowls and saucepans that littered the counter and stove.

She had begun preparations for this evening's meal early in the morning, right after Mrs. Manzer's nickel tour of the house and surrounding grounds. The first guests of the season weren't due to arrive until the weekend, still two days away, and additional employees would arrive at their leisure tomorrow. They were seasonal regulars, as were most of the guests.

According to Mrs. Manzer, Sharlie could have spent the day exploring the area or relaxing, but Sharlie had chosen to cook. The owner of the inn was driving down from San Francisco this afternoon, and she wanted to have a hot meal waiting for him, a meal that would prove beyond a doubt that she was equal to the task of cooking for this lovely inn.

Mrs. Manzer set the table that afternoon and planned to serve the meal herself, so Sharlie would have a chance to freshen up and change from her usual work uniform of jeans and an old sweatshirt into a dress.

Pushing her tattered sleeves up to her elbows, Sharlie took a dish of sweet butter curls out of the icebox and deftly arranged them to look like the petals of a golden flower.

Her stomach started to flutter with nerves as her dinner took shape. It was a relief when Mrs. Manzer bustled through the kitchen door and commenced serving the meal. Sharlie had to consciously refrain from following her out the door, arranging parsley and watercress sprigs on the plate. She wanted everything to be perfect.

Finally Mrs. Manzer came through the door to fetch the dessert, a rich chocolate gelato that was frozen into a ball and rolled in chopped dark and white chocolate. Sharlie placed the gelato on a small glass serving dish and surrounded it with a fresh raspberry puree.

Mrs. Manzer beamed. "Oh, I'm going to enjoy putting away leftovers around here. Everything looks so delicious. You come into the dining room now and have coffee."

"Now?" Sharlie plucked at the collar of her sweatshirt. "I'd better change first and clean up a bit. I smell like chicken."

Mrs. Manzer chuckled cheerily and brought an extra coffee cup and saucer down from a shelf. "You're fine as you are. But go freshen up if you want to. I'll tell him you'll be right along."

Sharlie nodded and headed for the back staircase, which led from the kitchen to the second-floor bedrooms. Before she reached the foot of the stairs, however, she turned. She didn't even know the owner's name. Mrs. Manzer had never used it. She opened her mouth to ask, but the housekeeper was already gone. Shrugging, Sharlie climbed up the stairs. She would find out soon enough.

Hurriedly, she undressed, washed off as best she could and ran to the closet to pull out a pale-blue skirt and blouse. Aunt Esther would not have approved. The outfit was far too sedate for Esther's taste, but it afforded the trustworthy, professional look Sharlie wanted.

When she returned to the dining room, she was unsure of how to announce herself or of how formal the owner of the inn chose to be, so she went to the dining room via the kitchen and knocked on the swinging door. Better to be too formal than too casual, she decided, but when no one answered, she knocked again and let herself into the room.

Sharlie looked first at the table. It was still beautifully set with flowers, the few remaining dishes and goblets clustered around one place at the head of the long table. A gray sport coat was tossed over the back of a chair, and a yellow tie was lying neatly on top of the coat. It looked like a lonely eating arrangement, and Sharlie frowned.

A movement by the wide French doors caught her eye, and she looked around. A tall form moved in from the patio.

The owner.

Without seeing Sharlie, he turned back toward the patio, closed the doors and remained staring out at the night.

The room was dimly lit, and Sharlie was tempted to back out without speaking. She knocked again on the door to get his attention.

"Excuse me."

When he turned and noticed her for the first time, a genuine smile warmed his face. "There you are. I was afraid you were going to hide all evening, and I wouldn't be able to compliment you on that wonderful meal you made for me."

Sharlie stood speechless.

"Some coffee?" He gestured toward the sideboard. "You make it very well."

Her eyes followed his hand, then moved back to his face. His expression was open and utterly guileless.

Jared Wright shrugged at her silence, a rueful twist to his lips as he crossed to the sideboard and poured steaming black coffee into a delicate china cup. "There's no need for introductions, of course, so why don't we sit down and—what is it they say?—" he chuckled "—have a friendly chat? How do you take your coffee?" He reached for the cream.

"No, thank you," Sharlie said, stopping him. "I don't want any coffee."

"From the tone of your voice, I gather that you don't want a friendly chat, either."

Sharlie stared at him. "We haven't had anything too friendly to say to each other so far."

Jared nodded. "Right. And you're obviously not feeling very friendly right now." He studied her face with sober eyes. "Okay, Sharlie, I realize that working for me isn't your idea of a dream job—"

"It's my idea of a nightmare. I don't have any intention of working for you, ever. I don't know why you dragged me out here, but you can just consider that meal a freebie, and we'll call it even." She pushed at the bridge of her glasses.

Jared studied her with interest. "You know, I just can't picture you as the girl who was swimming in champagne at Glen's party."

Sharlie looked at him ferociously. "What's that supposed to mean?"

"So touchy." Jared slid his hands in his pockets and shook his head. "I just meant that according to Glen you don't know a piña colada from a root beer float. Maybe you needed a little Dutch courage that night. Or do you just happen to like flirting, too?"

"What I like is none of your business." Sharlie's gray eyes narrowed behind her large glasses.

Jared shrugged. "I'm just curious by nature. You don't look like a habitual flirt. Was that a special night?"

"Look," she growled, intent on ending this conversation. "I happen to like to flirt. It didn't mean a thing. Goodbye." Turning her back on him, she shoved her way through the swinging door and into the kitchen. Jared was right behind her.

"Hold it. Hold it!" A large hand grasped her arm. With surprising gentleness, considering Sharlie was trying to yank her arm from his hold, Jared turned her around to face him. He raised his other hand in a gesture of truce. "You are right, and I apologize. There's no point in rubbing it in." His amber eyes were smiling kindly. "At any rate, Glen, his wedding cake—it's all water under the bridge at this point. Our goal now is to try to get along with each other, since we'll be working together."

His hands weren't holding her now; they were resting at his sides, and Sharlie crossed her own arms in front of her. She shook her head and used her coolest tone.

"We're not going to be working together. I'll be leaving in the morning. I'd leave tonight, but I have to repack."

Frowning, Jared sat on the oak stool near the center work island. There was a half-used box of raspberries still on the counter. He reached into it. "I hope you'll reconsider."

"I won't."

He popped the raspberry into his mouth. "You'll have to," he told her firmly. "We mailed you a contract, which you signed and mailed back to us. I have it in my office. Our first guests of the season will be arriving in two days, and I have neither the time nor the inclination to look for somebody to replace you. If you leave, I'll have to consider that a breach of contract."

Sharlie stared at him in amazement. He stood up and grabbed a towel to wipe the raspberry stain from his fingers. "If it makes you feel any better, you'll be working for my mother. It's her inn."

"Where is your mother?" Sharlie challenged.

"In Europe."

"Well then, she didn't hire me."

Jared grinned. "Oddly enough, it was her idea. Rather strange after the wedding cake fiasco, but my mother lives beyond the pale. Fortunately I, too, have an open mind, so you're getting a second chance."

"I don't want one."

"You're welcome. There now, see how easy it is to get along? Of course, it would help if you'd grab on to your end of the olive branch."

Jared turned to put the few remaining raspberries in the refrigerator, and Sharlie watched him stonily, unable to decipher his motives. "I want to know why you wrote to my aunt's catering firm."

He faced her squarely. His pale blue shirt emphasized his tan, and his teeth gleamed handsomely in a complacent smile.

Probably goes to a tanning parlor, Sharlie thought narrowly. She felt as white as cream in comparison.

"I wanted someone I knew I could trust. And you, Sharlie, cannot afford to be anything but scrupulously honest. Your aunt's reputation is at stake."

Sharlie smelled victory right around the corner. "Your power of logic," she stated calmly, "could fit inside a split pea. If I was willing to risk my aunt's reputation by deliberately lousing up a wedding cake, then why wouldn't I be willing to risk it again?"

"Ah, but you weren't willing to risk her reputation. Somebody ruined that wedding cake, but after careful consideration, I have concluded that it wasn't you." He stated his case with such infuriating confidence, that for the first time, Sharlie wished she had sabotaged the cake.

"Really, Sherlock? What makes you so sure?"

Jared grinned and took a step into her. Sharlie had to bend her neck to look up.

"Simple deduction, my dear Miss Kincaid. You cared about Glen. You must have cared about his opinion of you. And you don't seem like the fatal-attraction type. I don't think you would have done anything to hurt him."

His penetrating gaze dropped briefly as he rubbed his chin thoughtfully. "Do you still care about him?"

"Do you have a Dear Abby complex?" she returned. "I'm sure there are labor laws about prospective employers asking prospective employees things that are none of their business and which have nothing whatsoever to do with the job in question. Not that I am taking said job," she put her hand up to forestall any comments. "No," she said, gathering steam, "I am getting out of here, because I am not a puppet. You brought me up here under false pretenses, and I think I should report you to the Hotel and Restaurant Union or to the Bed and Breakfast Board...or to Clint Eastwood."

"He's not the mayor of Carmel, anymore."

"That's too bad. But somebody is, so watch your step." She nodded once to put a period on the conversation. "I'm going now."

She walked past him and stomped up the rear staircase to her bedroom. Her very temporary bedroom.

Jared watched her go. Picking up a dishrag, he carried it to the sink. He threw the towel over his shoulder, turned on the hot and cold taps and idly watched the water splash into the basin. He'd told Mrs. Manzer to make an early night of it, so it looked like the pots and pans were his responsibility. Squirting soap into the warm water and disinterestedly swishing it around to make suds, Jared grew moody.

Every meeting with Sharlie left laughter bouncing in his chest and frustration rumbling in his gut. She was right; they'd tricked her. On the other hand, staying in Orange County in close proximity to Glen and his new bride wouldn't have been good for her.

The image of Sharlie ruggedly trying to keep a stiff upper lip at the wedding glowed clearly in Jared's mind. He had the strong, abiding urge to protect her. He didn't want her to harbor feelings for his brother-in-law, because... because... dammit, because he didn't.

No, he decided again, grabbing a steel-wool pad and virtually scrubbing the shine off a pot as his mind wandered, she was too damn vulnerable. She was an open book, although he doubted that she was aware of the candor with which her face displayed her emotions.

He tried to remember his own infatuations. He frowned. The simple, sad truth was that after so many years of pursuing romantic relationships—when it had been convenient for him to do so—everything tended to blur together. Had his heart ever been broken? He shrugged. Briefly, perhaps.

Shaking his head, he wondered what women saw in Glen. His sister, whose level-headed dignity he had always admired, had practically tripped over her tongue because it was hanging so far out of her mouth when she met him. A small smile sneaked into the sternness of Jared's expression. In that instance, Glen had been obviously besotted himself.

Had Glen ever been interested in Sharlie? Jared had tried to pull that information out on a number of occasions, but Glen had always spoken of his admiration for her on a platonic level only. Glen didn't know if she'd ever dated once they left college, but in school, he said, she was the studious, single-minded type. She didn't date.

Putting the last of the pots on the counter to dry, Jared hurled the dishrag into the sink. Single-minded is right, he thought sourly. You would think she'd have wised up a lot sooner. What did she get out of it? He could remember a time when he'd wished for the kind of loyalty Sharlie had bestowed on Glen. He would have taken great pleasure in a relationship that consuming, a love that committed and pure. What's more, he flattered himself, he would have given as much as he'd received, and then some.

He turned to the wooden work island to see if he'd left anything uncleaned, then slapped the counter with the towel. Why was it that women were only happy when they were devoted to men who didn't know they were alive?

Disgruntled, Jared turned to grab a beer from the refrigerator and nearly tripped over Mrs. Manzer, who was standing in the middle of the kitchen with her robe wrapped securely around her. She was watching his movements with a surprised look on her pink face. Jared mumbled something incoherent, which Mrs. Manzer assumed to be an explanation, and stalked out of the kitchen.

A moment later Mrs. Manzer heard the front door slam. With a little shake of her head, she plopped herself down on the oak bar stool. She had known Jared since he was a boy, and she knew now that he would head for the beach to walk off whatever was bothering him. Lately he had been moodier than she had ever seen him. It was probably the effect of Gina getting married. She was younger than Jared, and although Jared never seemed to get involved seriously, and it was not a topic open for discussion, she was sure he was feeling some frustration. It wasn't good for people to be alone. After a while they got used to it.

Stifling a yawn, she decided to go to bed. It was early yet, but she would have a long day tomorrow, supervising the crew that was due to arrive. She knew them all. With the exception of Sharlie, they were all returning from last season. Sharlie, she was sure, would fit in fine. The smell of her cooking could win friends all by itself.

Thinking of the meal Sharlie had prepared for Jared reminded Mrs. Manzer that there was a potato and sweet-onion souffle right next to the dish of Burgundy chicken on the third shelf of the refrigerator. Sharlie had left the food for her, and Mrs. Manzer had planned to save it for lunch the next day, but no doubt there would be new delicacies to try tomorrow, and the chicken would go to waste. It would be a crime to throw out such tasty food. That settled, Mrs. Manzer grabbed one of the pans Jared had just scrubbed and commenced warming up her evening snack.

Chapter Four

Sunlight streamed in the window, slanting across the mirror and making it impossible for Sharlie to see herself in any but an honest light. She sat in her room and bade a silent farewell to the old Charlene Elysia Kincaid. She had come to several decisions last night, the first of which was to stay at the inn. Leaving would be the coward's way out. The new Sharlie Kincaid was no coward.

She had tossed and turned all night in the beautiful four-poster, so much so that Lotty had retreated to sleep on the floor for the first time in her life. But at least Sharlie had reached a conclusion about herself: she had to change. Everything had to change. Her clothes, her hair, her attitude. She required a complete overhaul, and the first thing to go would be her virginity.

Staring into the mirror in the clear light of day, Sharlie nodded again, vehemently. What good had her dratted virginity ever done her, anyway? She'd had it for twenty-four years now, a lifetime, and where had it gotten her? She knew more about making hollandaise than she did about men.

Give her a filet mignon and she would turn it into tournedos de boeuf; hand her a man on a silver platter and she wouldn't know where to begin.

And as for true love, she told herself insistently, forget it. It was possible that some people were not meant to find reciprocal true love. Perhaps in the greater scheme of things, some people were supposed to concentrate on their careers or give to the world in a different way, possibly by writing poems about celibacy or articles for *Monk's Weekly*.

She was going to have an affair. She would take the plunge, find out what all the fuss was about. Then, maybe, if she found someone she truly wanted to spend time with, she would become part of a couple for a while, have a candlelit dinner for two, go to a drive-in movie, go on a picnic. It would be nice just to walk into a movie theater and know there was a shoulder to snuggle into if she didn't like the film.

The only problem facing her was where to begin. She wasn't equipped to go on a manhunt. Particularly when the quarry was going to be something purely physical. Peering critically into the mirror, she tried to look objectively at the image that stared back at her. Pitiful. All she saw was plainness. How had she allowed this to happen? How had she shrouded a fundamentally romantic spirit in so much dullness? You had to work very hard to look this drab.

She had never used makeup to its best advantage... or clothes, either, for that matter. She was five feet, three inches tall and fairly curvy; that kind of body shouldn't be impossible to wardrobe. She would throw out her college pleats and lace collars and find something sizzling.

Sharlie felt more positive than she had in weeks. She would not run away. She would stand and fight for a passionate life... in a great new dress.

After cooking most of the morning so she could fill the freezer with make-ahead purees and soup stocks, Sharlie drove into town to shop.

* * *

It was a beautiful day to enjoy the myriad pleasures of Carmel. The coolness of the ocean breeze had yielded to summer sunshine, and Sharlie was tempted on numerous occasions throughout the day to call a halt to shopping and escape instead to the lazy peace of a sidewalk café and a very tall iced cappuccino.

But Sharlie was on a mission, and her single-minded pursuit of change was beginning to pay off. Already in her possession was a dress of iced-peach silk, matching shoes, and the most lacy, sexy lingerie Sharlie had ever laid eyes on. She had allowed the salesgirl at the beach shop to talk her into two bathing suits that would have sent her group at Weight Watchers into shock. Her bank balance was non-existent by noon, and she was rapidly approaching the modest limit on her one and only credit card. It was a very good day.

Three o'clock had come and gone by the time Sharlie sat in a chair at Jerry Michel's Hair Experience. She stared at the other customers as they were snipped, moussed and blown dry. Most of the women looked as if they had been to the beauty parlor earlier that day. Her eyes met her own reflection in the mirror.

"So, where were you when they invented the layered look?" she asked the woman who stared back. She was through marching to a drummer who always seemed to be a beat behind. After today, she would be as au courant as anyone.

As she sat in the chair, awaiting her transformation, her mind wandered through a scenario in which she bumped into Jared Wright on the street, he in his suave three-piece suit, she more than a match in her new clothes, new makeup, new hair.

They bump. They meet.

"Excuse me," he drawls smoothly, brown eyes drawn and held by the startling young woman in peach. She is sexy, she is self-assured. He can do little more than stare.

"Sharlie?" he utters, amazed.

"It's 'Charlene' now." She smiles coolly, without smudging her lipstick.

"You look...oh, wow...you look wonderful," he gushes, his suaveness utterly destroyed by her beauty.

"Thank you."

"Are you alone? May I buy you a drink?"

Sharlie smiles a little, but before she can cruelly say "In your dreams!" another man approaches. He is tall. Very tall. He is Tom Selleck.

"Ready, lovekins?" Tom inquires gently, taking her arm in his hand. Tom looks at Jared. "Who's your little friend?"

Sharlie glances down. Jared appears to be shrinking. "Oh, this is ... um ... hmm, I forget."

"Jared," the tiny man squeaks. He has shrunk to four-foot-eight.

Sharlie's lips curled with relish at the scene playing in her head.

"I'm sorry," she murmured aloud, answering the Jared of her imagination, "we're busy this evening." She smiled warmly at the thought of watching him shrink several more inches.

"Mademoiselle. Mademoiselle!"

Sharlie came to attention, snapped out of her reverie by the man standing behind her.

Jerry Michel frowned as he stared at Sharlie via the mirror. "Your pardon, but I do not work evenings. We will do your hair now, non?"

"Oh." Sharlie sat up in the chair. "Yes, of course."

Jerry Michel was already concentrating on the work ahead. He pursed his lips as he lifted sections of Sharlie's hair, letting the hanks fall heavily back into place. He shook his head. "Too long. Too dry. *Bor*-ing color. You brush?"

"Pardon me?"

"You have curly hair and yet you brush," he accused, clicking his tongue. "You must never brush."

"I'm sorry. I didn't know."

"Sorry don't mend split ends, non?"

"No." Sharlie shook her head.

There was little talk from that point on as Jerry began Sharlie's transformation from "too long," "too dry" and "*Bor*-ing," to short, silky and stunning.

"Shake," Jerry ordered after lightly blowing her hair with a diffuser and touching up the tips with a curling iron. He grabbed some mousse and ran it through her curls, twisting a ringlet here, adjusting a bang there to suit his taste.

When he was satisfied, he stepped back and swiveled the chair so Sharlie could see her reflection in the mirror.

Gone were the long, heavy waves that Sharlie was forever trying to control. A billowy cloud of thick curls took their place. Her hair was shorter—it barely brushed her shoulders in back—but it was full and feminine, and it glinted with subtle beige and golden lights when she turned her head from side to side. It was everything she had hoped for and more.

"My God," Sharlie breathed.

"Thank you." Jerry nodded. "Now, you buy conditioner, a little mousse, and no more brushing, yes?"

Sharlie shook her head. "No...I mean yes, no more brushing."

"Bien. Now I will show you how genius Jerry Michel really is, and you will tell all your friends."

With that, Jerry went to work again, and an hour later Sharlie left the salon feeling like a butterfly whose cocoon had been smashed to smithereens. Her hair was sculpted into a dramatic 1960's retro look. Her makeup was bold and glittering. Beneath the accoutrements, she glowed with the luminousness of confidence. Dressed in one of her new outfits, a tight black denim jacket and jeans, Sharlie headed back to the inn.

All was quiet when she entered the foyer with her packages. The inn seemed deserted until a pair of footsteps sounded on the circular stairway. Sharlie was completely unprepared for the sight that greeted her.

"My Lord, it is you!" Glen's exclamation rang through the large entry as he bounded down the steps toward her. He grinned broadly when he reached her, pulling her into his arms for a strong, quick hug. Sharlie clung to her packages.

"So, you're working for Jared."

"For his mother." Sharlie barely managed a nod as her heart started to pound. Glen was tanned and relaxed and more handsome than ever. "How have you been?" She uttered the first inanity that came to mind, but before Glen could respond, the library doors opened, and Glen's wife and brother-in-law entered the broad hallway.

Jared's face remained impassive, his voice stayed neutral, but his eyes missed nothing as they swept over Sharlie. "You're back."

Glen held his arm out for Gina to join him. "Look who's here, honey." He looked back at Sharlie. "We were afraid we'd have to leave before we saw you."

Sharlie held her breath. Visions of an irate bride holding a machine gun pointed at Sharlie's heart danced before her eyes as she remembered the cake fiasco. She looked at Gina, prepared to launch into an embarrassingly earnest apology.

Gina crossed to her husband and smiled at Sharlie without a trace of rancor. "I'm glad you're back. Jared was about to call out the National Guard." She looked at Sharlie frankly. "Sharlie, you look so different I'm not sure I would have recognized you. You look wonderful, though. Doesn't she look great, honey?"

"Yeah, yeah," Glen agreed readily enough. He studied Sharlie quizzically for a moment. "Have you lost weight?"

Gina slapped her husband on the arm. "Men never notice anything," she scoffed. "I could dye my hair green, and he wouldn't bat an eye."

Sharlie smiled limply. It was almost as hard to believe that anyone would ever overlook the beauteous Gina as it was to accept the obvious kindness in the stunning woman's expression.

The air had been sharp outside, but there was a soft, comfortable warmth in the foyer. The pleasing scent of mousse and hair spray mingled with Glen's cologne. Men and women.

Sharlie might have felt exhilarated, but the situation was so thuddingly anticlimactic. She had spent more days than she cared to tally, waiting for a glimpse of Glen, a look from him in her direction, a smile she could believe was meant for her alone. He had been oblivious to it all. She wasn't sure whether to laugh at herself, cry or begin a Time Wasted column in her yearly debit and credit log.

"Those packages are getting heavy." Jared's comment was a statement, not a question.

Sharlie did not resist as he took a few of her parcels and led her up the stairs to her room. He dropped the bags he was carrying on the bed, reached for Sharlie's and dropped those on the bed, as well. He walked to the desk, pulled the chair out to face her, and sat in it with his elbows resting on his knees.

"I was surprised you decided to stay. Mrs. Manzer said you cooked all morning."

Sharlie said nothing.

Jared nodded. He gestured to the packages. "Looks like you had a good time in Carmel." Sharlie had no answer for that, either. Jared rubbed his hands together. "Well, good.

So, any great plans for the summer? Any side trips you want to take?'' He waited. "Casseroles you want to try?''

One fat tear rolled down Sharlie's cheek before she could stop it.

Jared's hands stilled. "Sharlie," he murmured standing up and taking a step toward her. He had the damnedest urge to pull her back to the chair, set her on his lap and catch her tears with his finger. His throat was getting dry. "Why are you crying?''

"I'm having a poignant moment."

Jared's eyes widened. "A what?''

"A poignant moment." She walked to the dresser, yanked a pink tissue from its box and blew delicately. "I have them during major life changes." She spoke with forced dignity and glared at him over her Kleenex. "They're usually private."

She stood quietly, as if waiting to see whether another tear would come and not appearing to care one way or the other. Suddenly Jared felt utterly inexperienced with women.

He shook his dark head. "I'm sorry, but would you elaborate on why this is a poignant moment?''

Sharlie's nose twitched. She rubbed it with the tissue. She had no idea why she didn't feel any of her usual trepidation over giving people personal information. Ordinarily she would have thought twice about giving Jared the time while they were standing in front of Big Ben. She listened for the voice telling her to keep quiet, but it didn't come.

"Unrequited love is always poignant," she stated quietly. "I found someone appealing, but he never really saw me. That's poignant."

Jared considered her words. "I wouldn't take it personally," he said after a moment. "Glen isn't that observant. The truth is that for a poet, he's overly influenced by a pretty face and a good pair of legs."

"He married your sister."

"Okay, great legs. His poems aren't even that good."

"Then why do you publish them?"

"They sell. Not too well, but we might be able to get some greeting cards out of them. Some women go for schmaltzy verse." He eyed her suspiciously. "You're not one of them, are you?"

Sharlie gaped. "You've just managed to insult three people, two of whom happen to be your relatives."

"One is only by marriage. Shall I tell you what I think?"

"No, thank you."

"All right. I think that infatuation is not poignant." He looked at her very directly. "Infatuations do not lead to responsible, balanced partnerships. I think you were fortunate that Glen wasn't attracted to you. You would have rushed in and been stuck with someone with whom you would never have had a truly equal relationship. You know, one with give and take, meaningful conversations, an argument or two, maybe even some kissing."

"Thank you, Dr. Brothers," Sharlie said, staring at him grimly. She didn't know when she had heard a more logical—or condescending—appraisal of another person's feelings. "It's all so clear to me now. Tell me, what do you do in your spare time, write self-help articles for *Psychology Today?* Or don't you have any spare time after you've finished doling out your nickel psychoanalysis for the day?"

Jared frowned at her. "Your talents may be wasted as a chef."

"I agree. Why don't I quit?"

Jared seemed to consider the possibility. "No, I don't think so," he decided. "After all, I still have a responsibility to my mother. Where did you get your hair done, by the way? Don't get angry!" He held up a hand to ward off the verbal blow that was imminent and smiled a bit. "I just wonder why anyone would cut off all those curls."

Sharlie's hand went to the back of her head. She frowned at the change in conversational direction. "I didn't cut them all off. I'm wearing it up."

"Well, that's a relief," Jared sighed, as he continued to evaluate her new look. "Gina was right, you look so different I almost didn't recognize you."

"You don't know me that well," Sharlie shrugged. He was leading up to something.

"I said *almost*. The truth is, your image is printed indelibly on my mind. Curly hair, freckles, the dent on the end of your nose. You're unmistakable." He looked at her curiously. "If you were this attracted to Glen in college, why didn't you just ask him out?"

Sharlie raised her chin. She looked like Katherine Hepburn in *Adam's Rib*. "If I wasn't shy, I would have."

Jared gave a roar of laughter. "You're about as shy as a locust in a cotton grove. You've never been shy with me."

"Your gift for analogy is overwhelming. Maybe I've never been shy with you because I don't care what you think," she suggested sweetly enough.

"Maybe you just trust me."

Sharlie smiled civilly. "Like I'd trust Jesse James with a six-shooter in each hand. Like I trust the dentist."

Jared shook his head. "Ah, your gift for analogy."

He leaned close, and Sharlie kept her eyes on his mouth to avoid having to meet his gaze. When his lips touched hers, she gave a small start of surprise at the warmth and firmness of the pressure. The subtle, masculine scent of his after-shave floated around her, and she felt slightly dazed. Before she could decide whether to demand that he take his slimy paws off her or to kiss him back, the pressure of his lips decreased. He lifted his head and stepped away.

He seemed surprised and a little disconcerted by his own action.

"I can make your excuses when I go back downstairs. Glen and Gina will be leaving in a few minutes, anyway." Charlie didn't disagree, so he nodded and turned to leave.

"By the way," he said casually, pausing to look back at her, "you have a lovely mouth. With a little more practice you could even learn to kiss back."

He grinned, then turned and closed the door mere seconds before a shoe box sailed through the space his head had just vacated.

Chapter Five

As a risk-taking, fly-by-the-seat-of-her-pants gal, Sharli
was running neck and neck with June Cleaver.

At the moment, she was standing behind a picnic table on
the beach, fiddling with some doilies and trying to blen‹
ever-so-unobtrusively in with the pasta salads.

Since the evening Jared had kissed her, a couple of pro‹
found changes had occurred: one, when she stopped bein‹
furious with Jared, she realized that she had learned a ver‹
valuable lesson. She was not frigid, a point of concern whe‹
one was approaching twenty-five years of age and ha‹
found herself attracted to only one unattainable member o‹
the male gender in her entire life. Jared had unwittingly al‹
leviated her fears. His personality grated on her like sand‹
paper on a sunburn, but somehow when he kissed her, he‹
libido ignored her personal opinion. There was hope for he‹
yet.

The second change, and it wasn't so much a change as
reaffirmation, was that her determination to relieve hersel‹
of her sexual ignorance had become an obsession.

Watson Jameson, a short-story and mystery writer, had arrived for his annual work-holiday at the inn. He fit into Sharlie's plans perfectly. Watson was attractive and sophisticated almost to a fault, Sharlie thought, when she saw his expertly styled hair and the tan that was literally too good to be true. He had a raw confidence and sexuality that was almost tangible. He was, in a word, eligible.

While Sharlie set the stage for the Big Seduction, she wondered nervously who would be seducing whom. Watson started flirting before he unpacked. Unfortunately it wasn't as flattering as it might have been. Sharlie got the impression that Watson wouldn't know how to engage in conversation with a woman without flirting.

At Sharlie's suggestion, Mrs. Manzer planned a beach party for the nine guests and the crew currently at the inn. Sharlie prepared sweet-and-sour barbecued ribs and chicken, baked potatoes, corn and three different salads. She hollowed out a red cabbage and filled it with cole slaw, hollowed out a watermelon and left a carved handle of rind to form a basket, which she loaded with fresh, juicy fruits. Jared was working in San Francisco and would not be present to either commend her efforts or comment on her plans for Watson. It was a fair trade-off.

So now, here they were. The sun was dipping gently toward the line of the horizon, the barbecue was fired up, folding tables were set with food, and music caroled pleasantly from a cassette player. Laughter, splashes of water and shrieks of fun mingled in the warm, moist air.

So why wasn't Sharlie out there grabbing a little attention? Obviously a genetic problem: she was born more hermit crab than beach bunny.

Mrs. Manzer, resplendent in a sunset-orange muu-muu, scurried to the picnic table and clucked at Sharlie. "You come away from there now. You've been fussing over the food and the drinks all afternoon. Go on and have a swim before the sun goes down."

"Oh, that's okay," Sharlie assured the housekeeper, but when Mrs. Manzer tried to wrestle the basting brush from her grip, she decided to make a clean getaway.

"You know what," she prevaricated, "I will go in the water, but I'd better get some more chips and ice first. That way I won't have to worry about it while I'm swimming."

Pretending not to hear Mrs. Manzer's protest that there was still plenty of everything, Sharlie sped off, heading up the pathway that led to the inn.

She would rummage around in the kitchen for a while, maybe feed Lotty again and get back just in time to feed everybody on the beach.

As she let herself into the inn, a subtle depression settled around her. Why was the idea of a summer fling so much more appealing when it was being plotted in the privacy of one's own imagination?

She paused by a large mirror in the entry and squinted through her new contact lenses. She liked what she saw. Her face and shoulders were rosy and glowing from the sun. Her golden hair was tousled and curly from the breeze and the salt air. She looked flushed and healthy.

Her bathing suit, however, had been designed by a die-hard exhibitionist. The material itself was attractive, with lilac and pastel-blue splashes of flowers, but there was barely enough of it to make a decent scarf. It was cut high in the thigh, low in the back, and the sides were cut out from just under the bust to her hip. From the waist down, she was respectably covered by a filmy wrap-around skirt in a matching pattern.

By hook or by crook, she had kept that skirt on all afternoon. Watson had tried several times to drag her into the water, but Sharlie had been successful in begging off every time.

Successful? She frowned. Planning to have a summer fling while refusing to appear in a bathing suit on a public beach did not add up to a recipe for success. Not unless you planned to have an affair fully clothed. She shook her curly head. It was time to test her new liberation.

Tossing the skirt over the back of a chair, Sharlie headed for the kitchen. Shrugging her shoulders back, she added a bounce to her step as she pushed through the swinging door. Barely a foot inside, she stopped in her tracks to find the door to the refrigerator open and a person foraging through the contents.

Sharlie gave a grunt of surprise. Jared straightened and looked at her. She couldn't move or speak. He couldn't stop staring. She had been running away from the memory of his kiss, and now the memory caught up with her as his unabashed gaze wove a spell around them. He seemed tense and intent, familiar and a stranger all at once. After a moment he spoke.

"Fish eat your swimsuit?" Suddenly, the Jared she was used to was there, grinning incorrigibly.

"The saleslady picked it out." Good. A pass-the-buck comment.

Jared nodded slowly. "She made a good choice. It looks great on you." He smiled again, gesturing at the work island. "You caught me raiding your refrigerator."

Sharlie looked around her. His suit jacket was thrown neatly over a stool, and the makings of a boring sandwich stood on the counter. Another lonely meal.

"Where is everybody?" Jared pulled mustard out of the refrigerator.

"At the beach party," Sharlie said, watching him. "We're having a barbecue. You could come down to the beach...if you're hungry." It was the only decent thing to say. His family paid for the food.

"A barbecue?" Jared paused in the middle of slicing a tomato. He didn't bother to hide his relief at having to forego a bologna and cheese sandwich. "Are you sure there's enough?"

Sharlie nodded. "Plenty. We're having ribs."

"I love ribs. I'll go shower and change and meet you out there."

Sharlie told him where they were situated on the beach, and whistling, Jared went to change. Grabbing her skirt, Sharlie found herself retreating again, this time *to* the party.

Jared's appearance at the barbecue a few moments later surprised everyone but Sharlie. He manned the grill, and when it was time to eat, he caught Sharlie's eye and motioned for her to join him. He was sitting with the Jeffersons, an ebullient family who vacationed at the inn every summer. Without knowing precisely why she did it, Sharlie pretended not to notice him. She took her plate to where Mrs. Manzer sat with Watson Jameson and a young couple from Washington. She glanced up a few times during the meal to find Jared glancing back.

Sharlie was confused and uncomfortable. She had felt too much back in the kitchen when Jared stared at her. Naturally there was tension, and naturally there was pleasure that such a handsome man found her attractive in a barely clothed state. Naturally. But there were other feelings weaving their insidious way into her consciousness, and she didn't want them there.

As their meal was ending, Watson leaned close to Sharlie and whispered, "Care to take a walk after dinner?"

She agreed without hesitation.

As Watson covertly studied Sharlie's legs, Sharlie covertly studied Watson. He was indeed good-looking. But Watson was good-looking in a studied way. He worked at it and he seemed acutely aware of the results. On top of that he had more highlights in his hair than Sharlie. Still, he was prime romantic-fling material.

Distracted, Sharlie lifted a forkful of potato and cheese to her mouth. Little shreds of half-melted cheddar hung from her lower lip, and she stuck her tongue out to catch the cheese as it glued itself to her chin.

Feeling a blush coming on, Sharlie quickly poked the cheese into her mouth with her fingers. Her eyes involuntarily went to Jared. To her chagrin, he was staring, and a secret little smile warmed his face when their eyes met. Subtly, almost without any hint of suggestiveness at all, his tongue came out and dabbed at the corner of his mouth. Sharlie jerked her eyes away. His smile widened.

Sharlie reached for her cola, suppressing the urge to smash the aluminum, liquid and all, and lowered her eyes as she drank. Holding the icy can of soda in her lap, she stared down at it. To her shock—and total disgust—she was attracted to Jared Wright. Perhaps she was a woman doomed to be interested in the wrong men. Men like Jared didn't have flings with novices. They had full-blown affairs with women whose flirting skills had been honed in preschool. Even Glen, a poet who was supposed to possess a modicum of depth and should have known better, chose a girl who didn't know the meaning of the word *blemish*. Inside, Sharlie was still the girl with owl glasses, who blushed too easily.

In any case, she'd had enough futile anticipation to last a lifetime. A mingled sense of desperation and daring welled up inside her. Looking over at Watson's plate and seeing that he had finished his meal, Sharlie made her suggestion with a distinct note of bravery. "Want to take that walk now?"

Watson purred, "Absolutely."

It was the response she had expected from him. They rose and began their stroll down the beach. It was dark now, with only the glow of moonlight guiding their steps.

"I know a wonderful place I'd love to show you," Watson whispered, tickling her ear with his breath as he snaked an arm around her waist.

Even without experience in the game of seduction, Sharlie knew that was a very bad come-on line, but she had anted into this particular game, and she was determined to play it through.

"Lead on," she told him. Watson laughed softly and tightened his hold. Sharlie was sure then that in the convoluted and confusing language of flirtation, she had just told him that she was as interested as he was.

"I'm very attracted to you, you know."

Sharlie looked at the sand squishing between her toes. "That's good," she mumbled, "because I'm attracted to you, too."

Watson threw back his head and inhaled with appreciation. He turned Sharlie to face him and made a low gurgle of pleasure. "You don't mince words, do you, sweet lady? I like that." His fingers fluttered along her bare arms. "There's a great deal about you that I like."

Sharlie tried to will herself to relax. Watson was handsome and seductive, and she wanted to be seduced. But she felt more tense than responsive. Mentally she shook herself.

"Do you want me to tell you what I like about you, sweet lady?"

"Yes. Sure."

His fingers pressed into her arms. "Or should I show you?"

Drawing her toward him, Watson inched his face toward hers. His blond hair sparkled in the moonlight. Sharlie concentrated furiously on the golden locks that waved over his forehead. *Relax,* she commanded herself fiercely. *This is what you want, so relax.*

Watson's lips loomed ever nearer. The moment before they made contact with hers, Sharlie whispered, "Wh-what about that place you were going to show me?"

"Later," he breathed, his voice laced with concerted passion. "I'll show you many different places later."

His mouth fell in on hers, and at first Sharlie felt an immediate and illogical need for air. As Watson continued to kiss her, however, she closed her eyes and waited for the feeling to come...the dizziness, the heat, the stirrings of passion that were supposed to assail her at about this time. She waited, and when Watson's mouth lifted from hers, she decided she hadn't tried hard enough.

"That was nice. Let's do it again." Watson apparently found nothing to complain about. His mouth met hers again. This time Sharlie tried to get involved. Her arms crawled around his back, she moved her head, and their lips smashed together. He made a low groan deep in his throat, and Sharlie answered with a sound deep in hers. The little noises were so manufactured Sharlie didn't know whether to laugh or cry. She thought she might laugh.

When one of Watson's hands slithered down to reach for her breast, Sharlie's eyes flew open in surprise. She wasn't even remotely enjoying this, and Watson was trying to deepen the involvement. She knew that despite her longing for romance, for passion, for sexual experience, she did not want him to touch her like this. She tried to accept the caress for the purely physical experience that it was, but the intimacy of it seemed almost repulsive.

Mingled with the revulsion came a crushing disappointment. Something was wrong with her. Her libido had gone AWOL.

Sharlie heard something and thought it was Watson making noises in his throat again, but when he lifted his head and turned toward the sound, she felt an inordinate sense of relief.

She looked in the direction of the voice that was now clearly discernible and felt a jolt as she made out the tall and looming form of Jared Wright striding surely toward them.

"Damn." Watson grimaced at the untimely interruption of their fun. He pulled back from Sharlie, but only by a few inches. Sharlie, who had missed the heat of passion, now felt the heat of embarrassment flushing her skin. Watson caressed her waist openly, in full view of Jared.

"Jameson." Jared nodded curtly, but his eyes were on Sharlie. His expression said that he had seen everything and was not amused.

"Glad I found you." His jaw was clenched so tightly that his lips barely moved as he spoke. He turned to Watson. "Why don't you go back to the barbecue and have a piece of that cake Sharlie baked. I have a little something I need to discuss with my chef."

Watson laughed smugly. "I'm sure that can wait, Jared. Sharlie and I are having a little tête-à-tête of our own."

Jared visibly waged a battle for self-control. "Nothing that can't be finished later, I'm sure. In the meantime, Sharlie's working for me, and I'd like to speak to her."

Watson assumed that his status as a guest gave him a certain leverage. He refused to back down. "She can't be working now, Jared. We've all eaten. Besides, the poor girl's been slaving over our supper all day. She deserves a little R and R . . . and whatever."

The last words were spoken for Sharlie's ears alone. She cringed. She sincerely hoped that Watson wrote more creatively than he spoke. Her eyes fluttered to Jared.

A little pang of hurt and chagrin thudded dully in her stomach. She was an employee who had sneaked off for an evening rendezvous with one of his patrons. The situation was as sordid as it looked. Suddenly her libido wasn't nearly as important as erasing that look of censure in Jared's eyes. She wished more than anything that she had not walked off with Watson tonight.

Jared didn't wait for Sharlie's consent, nor did he concern himself with the feelings of Mr. Jameson. "Excuse us," he said without a hint of politeness, taking one of Sharlie's arms and firmly extracting her from Watson's grasp. Stunned, Watson watched them go, glaring impotently at Jared's back as he and Sharlie walked out of sight.

When they were alone on the beach, Jared let go of Sharlie's arm. He said nothing at all for a moment. Sharlie chanced a look at him and saw that he was waiting for her full attention, giving himself time to calm down in the interim.

He crossed his arms and nodded. "Very professional behavior."

Sharlie curled her toes around the cold sand. She said nothing.

"Your being the chef and initiating an affair with one of the guests might kill a few appetites, but other than that, you should be okay. You weren't planning to sneak Watson larger portions than the others are getting, were you?"

Sharlie didn't know whether to feel relieved or ashamed. The words were the teasing, facetious shots she was used to from Jared, but there was an unfamiliar edge to them now, and his eyes were cold. He was looking at her as though he didn't like her.

"I didn't initiate anything," she murmured in her own defense.

"Just jumped at the invitation?"

Sharlie didn't know what to say. All her adult life she had been waiting for a man to pay some serious attention to her, and Watson had paid it. Jared could never understand that. She looked at him now—the implacable set of his jaw, the thinned, disapproving line of his mouth. She was wondering how to wipe that damning look off his face, when an unexpected surge of indignation assailed her.

She pasted an innocent expression over her turbulent thoughts.

"You don't believe in affairs?"

The coolness in his topaz eyes yielded to consternation. Sharlie felt the first stab of satisfaction.

"This may be too personal, but what do you do for…um, you know…companionship? Don't you believe in dating, either?"

Jared shook his head in confusion. "Yes, of course I believe in dating. What are you talking about?"

"Oh, so you date, but you've never had an affair?"

"Yes, I— Wait a minute, what does this have to do with you and Jameson?"

Sharlie gathered steam. "On what grounds, precisely, do you object to a relationship between Watson and me?"

"On the grounds that he doesn't know the meaning of the word and apparently you don't, either!" Jared thundered. "What are you talking about, anyway? *Relationship,*" he scoffed. "You've known him a day and a half."

"Have all of your relationships been the meaningful, committed variety?"

"Yes, dammit, they have!"

"You mean you thought they were going to last forever? Every time?"

"Stop twisting this around. We're talking about you and Jameson."

"*You* were talking about me and Watson," Sharlie pointed out, the glitter of victory lighting her eyes. "I was talking about the old double standard. What's good for the gander is sleazy when the goose tries it."

Jared splayed one hand over his hip and used the other hand to rub his eyes. He looked handsome and intensely masculine in the moonlight. More than anything, Sharlie wanted to keep arguing with him. She wanted to know why he cared about her and Watson. She wanted to know exactly how many "committed" relationships he'd had.

"Watson and I will be discreet, if that's what's bothering you."

Jared tossed his hands up in exasperation. "Sharlie, get it through your head. You are not going to have a relationship with Watson. Do you know what kind of man he is? Jameson is interested in one thing and one thing only. He stays here for two weeks every year. Then he's gone until the next summer. *Two weeks.* Is that what you want? Because he's not some high school kid you can give two kisses to and then walk away from."

"I'm not in high school, either."

"Good, because now that I think about it, you wouldn't be safe there, either."

Sharlie trembled with indignation and frustration. She stared at Jared resentfully. What gave him the right to determine how she should live? What did he know about her loneliness? Suddenly Sharlie was assailed by an aching, bitter frustration. She had never known what it was like to be in arms like his, arms that must be as used to holding a woman as they were hanging by his side. Women had arms like that, too, arms that were comfortable holding a man, arms that were not always empty.

Safe was suddenly the last thing Sharlie wanted to be, and she told him so. His eyes narrowed and his mouth thinned when she said it. He had both hands on his hips, and the muscles in his arms flexed with tension.

"Jameson wants a quick affair. Is that what you're after?"

"Yes," Sharlie said, but her voice quivered with uncertainty when she said it. What she thought she wanted and what she was capable of were two different things.

"With Jameson?" Jared persisted. His tone was even, but the disapproval was too rich to be mistaken. His judgment of her spurred her on.

"Yes!"

The irony in that single, brave claim was her undoing. How could she have an affair with someone she didn't even want to kiss?

For years Sharlie had longed to know the experience of being close to someone. She had waited patiently and then impatiently to discover if being part of a couple was the joyful experience she had always dreamed it would be, if loving someone engendered the feelings of excitement and peace she had always dreamed that it would. Now she began to wonder if she would ever have the opportunity to find out. Her heart sank like a lead weight in her chest.

Sharlie was dragged from her thoughts when Jared had to repeat his question. "Are you telling me the truth? Is an affair with Jameson really what you want?"

"Yes," Sharlie said again, trying desperately to swallow the tears that filled her voice. "Yes, I do." But the lie filled her with frustration until she felt like a balloon that had been stretched to its limit and she thought she would explode from the confusion she was feeling. She shook her head as the tears slid off her cheeks and onto the sand.

She cried and hiccoughed, relinquished all dignity, and would have felt like a hopeless fool through it all if not for the arms that came swiftly around her, holding her surely and without hesitation.

Jared whispered to her to cry all she wanted, every trace of anger gone from the rich, deep voice that washed over and around her until she was enveloped in a cocoon of warmth and comfort. When at last she was quiet and had sniffed her last sniffle, Jared guided her to a small dune and sat beside her on the soft sand.

"Want to tell me about it?" he asked kindly, reluctant to push her.

"There's nothing to tell," Sharlie shrugged, searching for a discreet way to wipe her nose.

"There has to be something. Are you having another poignant moment?"

Sharlie started to glower, then realized that Jared wasn't being sarcastic; he was confused.

"I'm just crying over nothing."

"Girls don't cry over nothing."

"Don't be sexist. A lot of people cry over nothing."

Jared draped an arm over his bent knee and gazed out at the dark water. "Not you, though."

"Me?" That was a laugh. "I cry all the time. Over nothing at all."

"Did Jameson hurt you in any way?"

Sharlie glanced at Jared in surprise. He sounded so protective, like a big brother, all set to beat up the bullies. She smiled. "No, I wanted him to kiss me."

"I see." Jared digested the information. "You are attracted to him, then?"

"No," Sharlie sighed. Her eyes began to water again. "I'm not attracted to anyone."

Jared twisted to face her. "Sharlie, this is very confusing—"

"I know." She wagged her head forlornly. "Either men aren't attracted to me or I'm not attracted to them and that's that."

"You're saying this because of Glen?"

Sharlie sniffled, gave an eloquent shrug and stared silently out to sea.

"You are exaggerating, aren't you?"

A considerable silence followed. Finally Sharlie shrugged again.

"Watson found you attractive," Jared offered begrudgingly.

"That doesn't count. Nothing happened."

"All right, but it hasn't always been like that." Jared probed tentatively. His curiosity was killing him now, and indelicate, indiscreet, or downright rude as it might be, he had to ask the question.

"I mean, at some point, with someone, something must have happened." He peered at her closely. "Hasn't it? Sharlie," he said, his voice low and gentle, "are you a...?" He let the question dangle, hoping she would supply the missing word herself.

Sharlie turned her head to face him, her hair a soft, curling halo in the night. She gazed until understanding dawned. Her hand slapped the sand.

"None of your business! That is so typically male," she sneered. "You think that anyone who hasn't had thirty affairs by the time she's twenty is some kind of freak!"

"Aren't you almost twenty-five?"

"Ooh, you—" Momentarily speechless, Sharlie grabbed a handful of sand and flung it at his chest. "Let me tell you something, Mr. Smooth," she said when she found her voice, "lack of sexual experience does not mean that somebody is frigid. Nor does lack of opportunity denote lack of passion."

"Wait a minute, wait a minute!" Jared held out his hands. "Did I tell you to have an affair with Watson? How did I get to be such a bad guy? I just saved you from making one of the biggest mistakes of your life."

"What mistake?"

"Watson!" Jared hollered. "The man is no more capable of a real, committed relationship than a spider with a house fly."

"I have no desire to have a relationship," Sharlie informed him. "My present desire is to gain knowledge only."

"'Gain knowledge'?" Jared repeated incredulously. "What does that mean, you're in the market for an encyclopedia?"

"No, an affair. And you can take that shocked look off your face unless you want to tell me that you have never, ever, in your entire career as a carousing mass of male hormones, had an affair just because you felt like it."

Sharlie stared him down, and Jared had the grace to look uncomfortable. He stood, his hands searching for pockets in which to casually fidget. When he remembered that he was wearing swimming trunks, he balled his hands into fists and thrust them determinedly at his sides.

"I do not like the way you put that, Sharlie. But I will respond to it, because my answer may help you make some sense of what you're saying."

Jared took a couple of paces, stared hard at the sand and then out toward the ocean. "It is true," he began carefully, "that I have had relationships which did not culminate in, say, marriage. But I have always tried to explore the emo-

tional aspects of a relationship as well as the more..." His
hand stirred the air while he searched for his word.

"Smutty," Sharlie supplied.

"No—"

"Base...animalistic...physical..." she offered.

"Intimate aspects of a relationship," Jared finished, determined to treat this matter with the sobriety it deserved.

"Ahh," Sharlie nodded. "You knew their names then?"

"Yes, I knew their names!" Jared exploded in exasperation. "I knew a hell of a lot more about them than you
know about Watson. And it still wasn't enough, if you want
the truth. There is more to life than having a date on Saturday. Or a mindless affair to take your attention off what
you really want."

"Fine," Sharlie agreed. "I believe you. But I'll start with
the affair."

"Like hell! You don't know what you're doing. You admitted as much."

"That's why I'm going to do it. To find out what I don't
know."

Jared raked first one hand and then the other through his
chestnut hair. He lowered his head and sighed explosively.
So Sharlie was determined to have an affair. Looking at her
mutinous face, he was fairly certain that nothing he could
say tonight would change her mind; but he also knew—and
with far greater certainty—that she would embark upon a
meaningless pseudo romance only over his dead body. Or
Watson's.

Painting a deceptively bland look on a face that only a
second before was contorted with frustration, Jared held a
hand out to Sharlie.

"Okay," he said and pulled her to her feet.

Sharlie waited for him to elaborate on that *okay* as they
wound their way across the beach and up stony, sand-
sprinkled steps that led to the inn.

He didn't let go of her hand as they walked, and he didn't say a word.

When they reached the front door, Jared held it for her, and she passed by him into the foyer. Before she reached the stairs, he spoke.

"I'm sorry if I interrupted something with Watson that you didn't want interrupted. But I hope you'll give at least a little thought to what I said." He grinned. "After all, I am the voice of experience."

"A regular Johnson and Johnson," Sharlie quipped.

"That's *Masters* and Johnson."

Fascinated by the incredible expanse of skin that could turn beet red on Sharlie, Jared watched her whip around and stomp up the stairs to her room. Her irritation was evident in every step. She was going to get carpet burns on the soles of her bare feet.

Something stirred inside Jared as he watched Sharlie, and he was too old and too experienced to wonder what that something was.

"Lust," he muttered resignedly, crossing the hall to enter the library. Space to think was what he needed right now, space to think and a drink.

There was a decanter of amber liquor on his mother's old mahogany desk. Jared unplugged the crystal cork and sniffed. Sherry. His mother's only concession to keeping alcohol available for their guests. It would have to do. He poured a good shot into a too-dainty glass and downed it in one noisy gulp. It was either the sherry or a cold shower, and he didn't trust himself to be upstairs right now.

No doubt about it, there was something about that blond, gray-eyed, curvy pixie of a woman that made him want to—

"Lust," he mumbled again, knowing that was at least part of his motivation.

He took another swig of sherry to drown the feeling. If he was any kind of decent human being he would pull his mind out of the gutter where it was slithering and consider what Sharlie needed.

She had never had an affair before. Remarkable, but true. When it came to men, Sharlie was a babe in the woods, and there was a wolf like Watson behind every tree.

It wasn't just Sharlie's lack of experience that set her apart from other women, however. Jared rolled the crystal glass between his hands. The amber glow of the liquid reflected the fire growing in his narrowed eyes. Sharlie Kincaid was a unicorn, no doubt about that. For all her brave swagger about affairs and love for the sake of experience, Jared knew with unshakable certainty that when the cards were on the table, she would choose to spend her life alone before she succumbed to the temptation of intimacy without love. That particular fallout from the sexual revolution had left her unscathed—until now.

With a hearty thud, Jared set the glass on the desk. What she needed was not an affair, but a bodyguard. She needed a friend she could trust until the right man came along to sweep her off her feet.

Tapping a tan finger on his lips, Jared's musing brought a speculative gleam to his topaz eyes. Sharlie needed someone who could keep her out of the clutches of men who had sludge for scruples when it came to vulnerable women. She needed someone who could help her gain the confidence she needed, someone who could control himself. With time she would probably look upon that special someone as a real godsend.

Well, his mother hadn't sent him to Sunday school for nothing. He knew how to behave when he had to. And if his conscience served his purposes in the long run, well, all's fair.... Jared's smile deepened into a grin.

The first letter of business was to tell Watson where to keep his lips in the future. Jared's grin turned into a tiny, malicious tug at the corners of his mouth. The sight of Watson, who had always slithered better than he walked, putting his hands all over Sharlie made Jared's blood pressure rise to the boiling point. It would be a true pleasure to cut a couple of notches in the piece of soggy rawhide Watson called a heart.

Jared stretched his bare legs, cracked his knuckles and rose to his feet. Time to get to work. Somehow he sensed that being Sharlie's friend wouldn't be all fun and games.

Chapter Six

Jared hid behind the door to the kitchen and eavesdropped unrepentantly. Mrs. Manzer was playing her part very well, but Sharlie's obvious reluctance to take the bait was a little insulting.

"I'd go into town myself," Mrs. Manzer perfectly recited the lines Jared had given her, "but I want to supervise the cleanup in cottage B. Those children tracked in so much sand, you'd think they were trying to build castles right there on the floor."

"Well, I don't mind going into town," Sharlie prevaricated, her voice heavy with an implied *but* that Mrs. Manzer effectively overrode.

"I'd say you could take your own car, but Jared's going into town, anyway, and I want you to pick up some heavier cleaning supplies."

"Heavier supplies?" From where Jared was standing, he could hear the hopefulness in Sharlie's voice. "Well, if it's a mop or a couple of new brooms or something . . ."

"No, no, heavier than that," Mrs. Manzer insisted. "I need a...umm..."

A steam cleaner. Jared tried mental telepathy. *Say a steam cleaner.*

"A—you know..." Mrs. Manzer gurgled. "One of those whatchamacallits...uh...carpet vacuums with the, umm, liquid. Like they show on TV."

Close enough. Jared shrugged.

"Oh." It sounded like surrender. "Well, if you're sure Jared doesn't mind."

Mrs. Manzer laughed. "Oh, no," she spoke loudly, so Jared would hear her. "He won't mind at all."

"Fine then." The disappointment was clear.

Jared pulled his ear away from the door and frowned. He had known it would take some maneuvering to make her agree to spend the morning with him (much less the day, which was what he really intended) but this was downright insulting. After all, he'd only had her best interests at heart last night, and they had parted on pleasant terms. Well, on speaking terms.

"All right, you go get your things, and I'll tell Jared that you'll be ready in a minute," Mrs. Manzer called in increasing volume to tell Jared that the coast was clear. The final words were practically a yell. Jared grimaced. Subtlety was not her strong suit.

Sighing, he turned to head through the door.

"Okay, you can come in—" Mrs. Manzer pushed through the swinging door an instant before Jared started through on his side, and the resounding thud resulted in a sizable bump rising on Jared's previously smooth forehead.

Through a chorus of "Oooh, I'm sorry's" and "No, that's all right's" Jared managed to get to the sink and press a wet cloth against his throbbing skull.

"You did very well, Mrs. Manzer."

"Oh, I was happy to do it. I'm just surprised you two aren't getting along. She's such a darling person."

"Just a matter of a small disagreement. I'll get it all straightened out this afternoon."

"Well, I think that picnic is a lovely idea," she clucked approvingly. "And don't you worry about getting her back early, either. I have everything under control, and you can just take as much time with her as you like."

"Thank you, Mrs. Manzer," Jared mumbled, folding the washcloth and laying it in the sink. "I appreciate that." He was vaguely amused by the hint of suggestiveness he detected in her tone. "I'm going to pull the car around front now."

"You do that. I'll tell her you're out there. And I'll put some extra ice in the cooler for your head. And watch where you're walking now." Mrs. Manzer watched him fondly, thinking again that the picnic was a very good idea, indeed, though she didn't know whom he thought he was fooling. She hummed merrily as she got more ice for the cooler. Love was grand.

Upstairs in her room, Sharlie stood over her dresser drawer as she rummaged through the contents. She hurled an assortment of tops onto the bed from over her shoulder. Most of them landed on Lotty, who proceeded to fight them to the death.

Sharlie grumbled audibly until she found the peach cotton T-shirt that matched her peach jeans. She hadn't wanted to insult Mrs. Manzer, but domestic shopping with Jared Wright was not how she wanted to spend her day. She'd been up most of the night, tossing and turning and berating herself for giving Jared such a clear view of her neuroses. Even now she wasn't quite sure how he had tricked her into sharing more than one confidence that she should have kept to herself.

Moreover, after agonizing thought, she still wasn't sure whether to thank him for stepping in before her rendezvous with Watson got out of hand or whether to insist that he mind his own business from here on in. Watson's kiss al-

most made her wish her lips had been hermetically sealed,
but he was available and willing, and she was going to have
to get past this selective frigidity somehow.

Yanking the shirt over her head and tugging the zipper up
on her jeans, Sharlie decided that the best way to handle the
field trip with Jared would be to avoid all honesty and any
attempt at conversation. She could easily resist his clever
barbs, and she would not allow herself to be sucked into any
"meaningful" conversation.

Running her fingers though her curls, she shook her head.
They were only going to the hardware store. They probably
wouldn't say more than two words to each other, anyway.
As for Watson, she could put off any decision about a relationship with him until . . . well, at least until she saw him
again.

That settled, she fluffed her hair and headed downstairs,
prepared to spend a cool, quiet—if not silent—hour or two
with Jared Wright.

"I'm not hungry," Sharlie insisted stubbornly as Jared
cruised the car along a majestically tree-lined street.

"Then should I be taking that growling personally?"

"Take it any way you like, because I'm not hungry."

Jared sighed. "All right, Sharlie, fess up. You've argued
about everything there was to argue about since you got in
the car."

Sharlie looked surprised. "I have not. Just because I
happen to dislike country music?" She'd made him change
the station seven times.

"You also have strong opinions about green broom han-
dles, floral room freshener, yellow soap—"

"It smelled like bananas."

"You haven't liked a single thing all morning." Jared
passed a hand over his face. Fortunately much of his humor was still intact. "At least we don't have to worry about
you suppressing your true feelings."

No, not when it comes to something as monumentally important as floral room freshener, Sharlie thought morosely. He was right. All morning long, she had challenged him on anything and everything. She was really a very pleasant, amenable person when she wasn't with Jared. She rarely ventured a contrary viewpoint unless she knew the person she was with very well—for say, ten or twelve years. What really threw her, though, was Jared's uncrackable equanimity throughout the morning. He met every one of her contradictions with smiling acquiescence to her point of view. He was determined to be friendly.

Jared pulled the BMW up to the curb. He cut the ignition and turned to Sharlie.

"You may get out of the car now," he told her happily, opening his door and swiftly moving around the car to her side.

"Where are we?" she asked, sinking back into the bucket seat.

"We're going to have lunch."

Sharlie stared past Jared to the wide expanse of lawn and the pretty ranch-style structure trimmed in flagstone.

"This is a restaurant?"

Jared looked over his shoulder. "No, this is a house." He pointed across the street. "That is a *park,* and we're going on a *picnic.* Coming?"

"Just us?"

"I didn't bring that much food, but if you see somebody you'd like to invite..." Jared shrugged impatiently. "You are one hard person to try to be friends with, you know that?" He sighed, then smiled engagingly. "I'm trying to apologize for overstepping myself. We ought to be able to be friends if we're to work together. I distinctly remember learning that in grammar school. And we're considerably older than school age."

"I'm only twenty-four," Sharlie retorted, but his charm was working on her.

Jared grinned. "Well, these old bones are growing tired from running errands, and I get cranky if I'm not fed at regular intervals, so what do you say we go stake out a claim under one of those trees?"

With some trepidation, but an increasing appetite, Sharlie followed Jared to the park and watched while he spread a blanket on the ground and pulled out a picnic that could have persuaded Sitting Bull to call a truce. There was sliced prime rib with horseradish sauce, tiny kaiser rolls and three kinds of cheese, including a small wheel of Camembert covered with sliced, toasted almonds. There were English tea biscuits, scones studded with currants, and a small pot of strawberry jam. Plums and red grapes and the fattest chocolate chip cookies Sharlie had ever seen were dessert.

How could she help but be impressed with such a thorough effort? She enjoyed every bite and every moment of the picnic. Happily, she bit into her second cookie.

"Everything was wonderful. Why isn't Mrs. Manzer cooking for your mother's inn?"

Jared licked chocolate off his thumb and stretched out on the blanket. "Mrs. Manzer doesn't like to cook on a regular basis. Anyway, I made the cookies. I remembered that your cat has a sweet tooth. Figured it might run in the family."

"Very funny." Sharlie threw a grape at his head. "Where did you learn to bake?"

Jared crossed his arms behind his head, hooked one ankle over the other and gazed up into the shady world of an elm tree. The dappled afternoon sunlight filtered through the trees and picked out the golden strands in his chestnut hair. His face had the relaxed, contented look it had worn since they sat down to the picnic. He seemed happy to be where he was, and Sharlie realized with some wonder that she was feeling rather relaxed herself.

"Come on," she said, "who taught you? Your mother?"

"Nope. A girl I was in love with."

"Really?" If he stopped talking now, she would kill him.

"Yep. She had coal-black hair, the softest skin I'd ever seen, dreamy eyes—"

"Dreamy?"

"Yes, dreamy. Her eyes were brown...like cocoa. Ah, she made the best chocolate chip cookies I'd ever had. I was in love as soon as I tasted one."

"What was her name?"

"Dora Krupp."

Sharlie gaped at him. "So what happened with you and Dora?"

"I outgrew her."

"Lovely," Sharlie chided. "Don't you think that's a rather cavalier attitude?"

"Not at all. She was more suited to her husband than she was to me, anyway. Deep down, I think I sensed that all along."

"You were in love with a married woman?"

Jared picked up a twig and rolled it between his teeth. "She loved me, too."

"That must have been very painful for you." It must have been even more painful for Mr. Krupp. Sharlie found that she was intensely curious about the woman who had swept Jared off his feet with her chocolate chip cookies and cocoa eyes.

"How did you two meet?"

"In school."

"College?"

"No."

"Graduate school? You have an M.A.?"

Jared shook his head. "Grammar school. I have a terrible sweet tooth. She brought cookies to her classes once or twice a week. She's the one who taught me to play nicely with the people I work with."

Sharlie clenched her teeth. The muscles in her jaw bunched, and her upper lip began to twitch. "She was your teacher?"

"Taught me everything I know about puppy love."

"You crud." Sharlie began slowly, letting her irritation build. "You think you're funny? You rat! I was beginning to feel sorry for you. I actually credited you with a real human emotion."

Her anger didn't bother him a bit. "It was a real human emotion," Jared argued reasonably. "And you should feel sorry for me. I was young and easily hurt."

"By a juvenile crush," Sharlie dismissed.

"By a relationship and emotions that were very real to me at the time," Jared countered firmly. "It might not have meant anything to her—I'm not even certain she knew that I had a crush on her—but to me she was everything that could make me feel happy and secure."

"How old were you?"

"I had just turned twelve. And I wore glasses, and I shuttered. Badly," he responded to her look of surprise. "I felt like the world's first preteenage failure. I figured no one would ever look at me as kindly as Mrs. Krupp—or make a better chocolate chip cookie. It took me a long time to get over her. It took me a long time to find the courage to get over her and to focus my attentions on someone a little more available."

Sharlie said nothing for a time. She examined Jared's profile, his still-relaxed mien. He hadn't turned to her for more than a second or two while he recounted his passion for Dora Krupp, but Sharlie had the keen impression that she was being scrutinized nonetheless. Obviously the moral of the story was that she should honor, but move beyond, her feelings for Glen, feelings which she would eventually come to regard as a "crush." How was she supposed to respond to parallels as blatant as the ones he had drawn?

"I am over Glen," she asserted into the silence, watching Jared closely to gauge his response. She had liked him today, really liked him. She was getting over Glen, and it seemed important that Jared believe that.

Saying nothing for a moment, Jared lay gazing thoughtfully at the rustling leaves and the sky beyond. He turned and sat up on his elbow.

"Was I that subtle?" His infuriating grin returned.

"Like a lead pipe."

"Ah, well. I just want you to know that these things take time so you won't rush into anything."

"When did you get over Mrs. Krupp?"

"A year and a half ago."

Sharlie laughed at the woefulness of his expression. "Obviously I heal faster."

"I don't know. Jumping into Watson's arms on the rebound would seem to suggest otherwise."

Sharlie leaned over to tug on a mound of grass, pulling up several green blades and a good hunk of dirt. "Being attracted to Glen—at one time—and having a relationship now are two totally unrelated topics."

"If you had someone specific in mind, I might be inclined to agree with you. But you said you're just interested in 'experience.'"

Sharlie nodded. "So?"

"So, what's the rush?"

"Rush?" Incredulous, Sharlie slapped the blanket with the flat of her hand. "I'm almost twenty-five years old! You think I'm being precocious? I would at least like to know what I'm missing before I have to give it up for old age."

Jared laughed. "But jumping into bed with the first available—and, may I add, semicapable—male is not the answer. Some girls still wait for marriage," he reminded her.

"Yes, and they marry when they're fourteen," Sharlie scoffed.

Jared eyed her in the dappled light: the stubborn pout settled on her lips, the wavy hair, the smattering of freckles that rambled beautifully across her nose and cheeks. She was wearing her glasses today, and they perfectly framed her clear gray eyes and skipped adorably down her nose when she tilted her head.

He was sorely tempted to offer his own services in her quest for experience, but that would be like buying the ham hock when you could have the whole hog.

A grin poked at the corner of his mouth. Better keep that particular analogy to himself. Twirling the twig between his teeth, Jared rolled onto his back.

"I still don't understand," he said aloud. "Why have you waited so long to become involved with someone?"

Sharlie started to shrug the question away, but reconsidered when he turned his head back to face her. The look in his eyes was as straightforward as his question had been. *It's none of his business,* Sharlie told herself, her self-defense mechanism kicking in as it usually did, even as the urge to confide in Jared asserted itself. But in the instant that he turned to her with such clear acceptance on his handsome face, she knew she could trust him with whatever information she chose to divulge.

"I believe in true love," she began, and at the first hint of the encouraging smile that creased his face, she decided to tell him the whole truth: the frustrating years of adolescence, mooning after Glen, the growing fear now that if she waited for true love she'd be waiting forever.

Jared listened to it all with a calm, silent attentiveness. He said nothing when Sharlie was finished, and she hugged her knees to her chest, waiting impatiently for him to comment.

"Well?" she finally demanded when no response seemed forthcoming.

"I wasn't sure you wanted an opinion. You might not like it," he warned.

"Go ahead."

"Okay." Jared rolled to a sitting position, crossed his legs Indian-style, and rested his elbows on his knees. "I think it's rash and more than a little foolish to have an affair with someone just to put a notch on your belt."

"That's not what I'm trying to do. Besides, men do it all the time."

"Chauvinist."

Sharlie opened her mouth to rebut, then shook her head. "Never mind. You couldn't possibly understand, and I don't have the time to explain it all to you."

"Of course you don't," Jared agreed sympathetically. "You have a manhunt to get underway. Very time-consuming. But because I'm a nice guy—and definitely not a chauvinist—I'm going to do you a favor."

Aware that he had her curiosity piqued, he plunged ahead. "Now, admittedly you don't have a lot of experience with men. I, on the other hand, have been a man for thirty-three years. I know a great deal about us, and I can smell a skunk like Watson a mile off."

"So?"

"So I'm going to help you. You like artist types. We get a lot of them up here in the summer, and I know quite a few of them personally. I'll just steer you in the right direction. You need someone very special for this first experience . . . even if it is romance for the sake of sex."

"Wait a minute—"

"Love to acquire practical knowledge."

"Okay, hold it—"

"A notch on the belt of experience. You still need the right kind of guy. Definitely not a worm like Watson."

"Boy, you really like Watson."

"We're like fraternity brothers. So what do you say? I'll give you the background on these guys, my unbiased opinion, since your mind is obviously made up, and you're definitely going through with this—right?"

"Right."

"All right, then. I'll give you my unbiased opinion, and you make up your own mind from there. How does that sound?"

She hated every word of it, but found herself agreeing automatically. "Fine. Why do you want to do this?"

"Hmm." Jared frowned as he thought about it. "We're friends already, aren't we?"

Sharlie shrugged, then nodded slowly.

"Good." Jared smiled, satisfied with her lukewarm confirmation. "That's why. Also," he said, and his expression sobered a bit, "it's very hard to be pals with someone you're just having sex with. I'm telling you this as your friend now. You'll probably need someone you can talk to when you feel too awkward to talk to loverboy. So at least you'll be able to feel comfortable with me."

He smiled a big, reassuring smile, and Sharlie smiled back, definitely not reassured.

As they packed the picnic basket and folded the blanket, working to Jared's whistled rendition of "Bridge over Troubled Water," Sharlie had the disturbing feeling that she'd just been duped. He said he was going to help her, so why did she feel like she'd been talked into joining a convent? She eyed Jared suspiciously. He was working happily, whistling off-key with a guileless expression on his masculine face.

Sharlie shook her head and stuffed a wedge of Gouda into the hamper. She would not back down. An affair was what she wanted . . . correction, what she *needed* . . . and an affair was what she was going to have.

Chapter Seven

"Not so far, not so far!" Jared yelled, then threw his Oakland A's cap on the damp grass and ran for the softball that was soaring high over his head. He undershot it by about a foot, raised his glove up and back and fell smack on the ground. He caught the ball.

"Did you see how far that went?" Sharlie shouted joyously, skipping to where Jared sat on the grass. "I can't believe it. I've never been able to throw a ball. That was great!"

"You're supposed to throw it *to me,* Sharlie," Jared reiterated, rubbing his sore neck. "I thought we went over that."

"Okay," Sharlie agreed happily. "Get up, and I'll throw it again."

"I'm not sure I can take it."

"Sure you can. I never used to be good at sports, but you know what? I think I might be a natural athlete at heart. What do you think?" She plopped down on the grass next to him. "You know, I think it's because I was always self-conscious before. I always thought I'd drop the ball or miss the hoop or something. This grass is wet.''

"Yes, it is.'' Jared agreed.

"I think you should have said something.''

"Do you?'' Jared glared at her.

Sharlie shrugged, a mischievous quirk twitching at her lips. "No reason for both of us to get wet.''

Jared growled menacingly, moving toward her.

Sharlie put up a hand to ward him off. "Whatever you're thinking, just remember that I'm wearing white, and white takes grass stains very—aaahh!''

Sharlie was up and running as Jared lunged for her. She felt as carefree as a puppy as she raced around the tree with Jared hot on her heels. She swerved first right, then left, as he'd taught her when they'd practiced football the week before.

When he caught her and tackled her to the damp ground, Jared made Sharlie agree to have hot dogs and ice-cream sundaes for dinner.

"Don't move!'' Sharlie slapped her pencil against the paper. "If you move, I'll mess up the mouth.'' She let out her breath on an exasperated hiss as Jared obligingly twisted back into position.

"I saw a lizard.''

"Just leave it alone,'' Sharlie ordered. So far, Jared had fidgeted in order to watch a squirrel, a family of ants and what he swore was a hawk. "This must be what it's like to draw children,'' she grumbled into her sketch pad.

"I heard that.''

"You were supposed to hear it. Now sit still.''

"I think I'll see what you've done so far.'' He got up to stroll to where Sharlie sat with her sketch pad.

"That does it!'' Sharlie tossed her pencil to the ground and threw the pad of paper on top of it. "I am not drawing you. You're impossible.''

"Now, don't get all hot and upset," Jared soothed, placing his hands on Sharlie's shoulders. "You're taking it too seriously. You didn't even glance at the hawk. If you show me the picture, I'll go sit down, and I promise not to move again until you tell me to."

"You can move all you want, because I'm not drawing you again. You couldn't sit still for more than two minutes if you were Crazy Glued to the grass."

Jared frowned. "You're right. Maybe if I had something to do."

"Why don't you read something? You must have a lot of manuscripts lying around, waiting to be published."

"That's true. But that's an extension of work. I usually do that late at night."

Sharlie cocked a brow at him. So, that was what he did late at night.

They'd been spending a considerable amount of time together over the past weeks. Jared had been making the drive from San Francisco on a regular basis, claiming mental burnout and a need for a more relaxed atmosphere. He cajoled Sharlie into helping him relax by playing softball, walking on the beach, throwing a Frisbee, and exploring tide pools. She had enjoyed herself so much each time, had felt so peaceful and buoyant that soon she started to waylay Jared to go on picnics, explore shops in the area or just chat.

She had changed in some way since she had come to work for him. She didn't know when she had changed, or how, or even what the change was, precisely; she knew only that she felt profoundly comfortable with Jared and with herself. It was a good feeling, an exhilarating feeling, as was the knowledge that in Jared she had one very good, very sincere friend.

The only niggling annoyance was that Sharlie had absolutely no idea what Jared did with his nights. Their friendship was restricted to the daylight hours, after which Jared would closet himself in his library to remain undisturbed the rest of the evening. Or, more often than not, he would drive away in his racy BMW to return with the engine grumbling up the driveway late, late at night.

Because Jared never offered any information as to where he went or what he did or why he hadn't spent more than one or two evenings with her since their tandem plunge into friendship, Sharlie remained stubbornly opposed to asking him. If he wanted her to know, he would tell her. Wouldn't he? What drove her up the wall was that she was left twiddling her thumbs at night while he did…whatever it was that he did. Being alone had never bothered her before; but it started to rankle that she was alone night after night, when there was someone nearby whose company she would have enjoyed.

Reading wasn't as engrossing as it used to be, the television failed to engage, and Lotty had made the entire inn her playground. So Sharlie started working at night, preparing as much of the next day's soup stock and baked goods as she could. She told herself that she was merely filling her evenings and being fabulously organized, but the undeniable truth was that with less to do during the day, she had more time to spend with Jared.

Sharlie looked at Jared now. He was sitting on his haunches, studying her sketch. His hair was ruffled by the breeze, and his brow was furrowed in concentration. She often caught him with that contemplative, absorbed look on his face, and, as always, it made her smile. He looked like a boy, so engrossed by something as simple as a drawing of a tree or a rock. Sunlight was reaching to them through the trees.

"So, what would persuade you to sit still?"

Jared looked up. "You could promise to make me fudge ice cream."

"I tried that an hour ago, and you went for the lizard. How about a book?"

"You're going to write me a book? It had better be a best-seller."

Sharlie shot him a long-suffering glare. "Why don't you read while I draw you?"

Jared considered it. "Actually, I wouldn't mind reading *The Secret Garden* again. This place reminds me of a secret garden, anyway. And you remind me of the heroine."

"Great," Sharlie agreed. "What's *The Secret Garden?*"

Jared fell back on the grass, his mouth agape in disbelief. "You're an illustrator, an artist, a member of the human race, and you don't know what *The Secret Garden* is?"

"I know it's a book."

Sketch pad in hand, Jared rolled to his feet. Handing Sharlie her tablet, he put one large hand on either side of her face. His fingers were warm and gentle against her skin, and Sharlie's heartbeat started to quicken. She fidgeted nervously.

Jared pretended not to notice her confusion, but his eyes twinkled. "Come with me. This is one gap in your life experience that we can easily fill."

Taking her hand, he led her off. A short time later they were back in the garden, positioned comfortably under an impossibly beautiful jacaranda tree. Sharlie bent diligently over her drawing as she tried to capture the sight, the sound, the nuance of Jared on this perfect summer afternoon. His voice fairly sang with the words of the novel he was reading. His obvious love of the story and his strong desire to share it with Sharlie warmed her as fully as the sun that poured gold all around them.

Sharlie listened as she drew, and the crystal blue of the sky yielded gracefully to pink and lilac, then to a deeper, more insistent shade of violet before the duo roused themselves and retired for the day.

To leave the story or the good feelings seemed an impossible task, so they raided the refrigerator, made a whole pot of hot cocoa and escaped to the library. There Jared continued the story while Sharlie sat on the plush carpet with her feet tucked under her, her back against a chair and a tissue clutched in her hand to mop her tears as she listened in rapt and devouring attention to the final pages of the story.

Jared finished the book with a sigh, and Sharlie blew noisily into her Kleenex.

"Why are you sad?" Jared leaned over and wound a curl gently around his finger.

"I'm not," Sharlie sniffed, shaking her head. "I'm happy. It's just so beautiful." She pressed the tissue to her face as another sob rose to her throat. Jared gathered her into his arms, murmuring soothingly.

Sharlie hated to cry in front of people; she was an unattractive sobber, and she usually poured enough tears to fill a small hot tub. But the book was so perfect, and it touched a responding chord in her, just as Jared said it would. Besides, Jared understood.

Sharlie smiled a watery smile against the fisherman's sweater into which she was pressed. Jared always understood. She relaxed in the strong arms that circled her. Her palm pressed against his chest, and she felt his steady heartbeat. He was so warm. She could feel the warmth through the rough sweater, as though her hand were touching the hairy chest beneath. She breathed in and filled herself with the scent of him. She had never felt so calmly, so peacefully alive. Life seemed to be all around her now, in her.

Frances Hodgsen Burnett's novel was right. Aunt Esther had been right. Life had to be pursued actively, with faith and with a full heart. Sharlie was learning that this summer, at long last. She felt more relaxed and comfortable with herself than ever before. When she allowed love into her life without fearing it, love came.

She pulled her head away from Jared's chest and gazed at him through the warm and lovely curtain of her thoughts.

Deep affection filled his eyes as he looked at her. His handsome mouth curved.

He spoke softly. "My buddy's a soft touch."

Sharlie frowned, and then her heart started pounding—hard. Her thoughts and his words seemed to pulse in her brain with every beat. Love? Had she fallen in love with her "buddy"? Her mind scrambled in cold anxiety to examine how she felt when Jared held her, when he read to her, when they talked...when he held her...when they played ball, when they laughed..and when he held her...when they picnicked, when they shopped...when he held her.

Damn!

Sharlie shook her head ferociously to disengage the thoughts. Her dreamy gaze grew brittle.

Jared looked at her in concern. "What's wrong?"

"Nothing. I thought you were going to find me a boyfriend."

Jared's face was now a bland mask. His hands burned her back. "Where did that come from?"

"I've been thinking about it. It's been weeks since you said you were going to help me." Buddy, buddy, buddy.

Jared rose and collected their cocoa cups, depositing them on the silver tray. He crossed to the fireplace, his thoughts tucked behind the hooded, neutral expression on his face.

"Still interested in something brief?"

Sharlie was momentarily stymied. She sensed a judgment lurking behind that question, but Jared's voice was as even and cool as the look on his face. The truth was that she wasn't certain what she needed or wanted anymore, but some perverse part of her made her answer in the affirmative.

"Yes. I think brief would be best, a good way to start. Assuming, of course, that I'm going to continue."

"Oh? Weren't you planning to continue?"

Sharlie shrugged. "I may. Or I may not. I'll see how I feel about it."

"What about love?"

"I tried it, it didn't work out. If it happens, it happens. If not..." She shrugged again.

Jared scowled at her. "Don't be ridiculous, Sharlie. Do you know how dangerous a series of affairs can be in this day and age? The era of the glorified casual encounter is behind us now."

"Oh, yeah? What does that make me? Just fresh out of luck because I was a late bloomer?" His brotherly condescension inflamed her, partly because he was right. She hadn't thought this through. But his tone spurred her on, and her cheeks flamed. "There are still plenty of relationships based on something other than love. And I'm going to have one before my libido shrivels up entirely!"

Jared looked startled a moment, then his head fell back, and the room rang with his laughter.

Sharlie's jaw tightened. "Don't laugh at me, Jared."

"I'm sorry. It's just that I have a feeling your libido will be fine." He sobered and looked Sharlie square in the eye. "All right. You want a date, you've got a date."

Chapter Eight

If the pin from this corsage sticks me one more time, I'm going to rip the flowers off and stuff them up your nose, Sharlie thought, smiling sweetly at her dinner companion, Christopher Robin Seton III.

Christopher Robin's parents obviously suffered from a Winnie-the-Pooh complex and had christened their son accordingly. It was unfortunate, because Christopher Robin had enough problems, given his nervous blink, his tendency to bump into things—knocking them to the floor with alarming frequency—and a little acne problem that had gone unattended.

Christopher Robin blinked at Sharlie through his glasses. She jabbed her fork into her lamb chop. An hour and a half and they were only on their entrée. Oh well, after another half hour they should be through with dessert; then Sharlie could plead a headache or severe gastrointestinal disorder—which Christopher Robin would no doubt understand, as he had been regaling her with his intestinal troubles since the soup course. They would go back to the inn, and

Sharlie would say good-night and goodbye. Then she would find Jared Wright and snuff him out like the bug he was. He said he would find her the perfect date, but little did Sharlie know when Jared uttered those immortal words, "Trust me," that she would be spending an entire evening opposite an eligible male and be able to think of nothing more than plotting the demise of her sneaky, double-crossing friend.

If Christopher Robin was Jared's idea of the perfect—or even appropriate—man to initiate her to the joys of romance, then how did Jared perceive her? Christopher Robin had barely uttered three words since they started eating, and before that his topics of conversation had been restricted to past and current health problems—his; dating history—hers, it was a short conversation; and the study of rock-dwelling insects as a hobby—definitely his.

Christopher Robin and his parents were annual guests of the inn, and Jared was ecstatic when they arrived. He hastily arranged this dinner date. Jared was nowhere to be seen, of course, when Sharlie met Christopher Robin for the first time, in the foyer at seven as prearranged. If she saw Jared now, she would—

Sharlie blinked. Either her mind had conjured the image of Jared in such detail that she was having an hallucination, or Jared was standing in the entry of the restaurant at this very moment. When the woman at his side moved close to him, murmured something and then doffed her coat to reveal the most stunning, slinkily clad figure Sharlie had ever seen during prime-time hours, she knew that she wasn't hallucinating. She never would have conjured this creature for Jared. He didn't deserve her. Sharlie's fork missed her mouth. Mint jelly slithered down her chin.

A little cough from across the table barely drew her attention. Christopher Robin spoke. "Excuse me, but you have a bit of mint jelly—"

"I know," Sharlie snapped, then nodded to Christopher and softened her response. "Thank you very much, Christopher Robin."

He smiled and blinked, then returned his attention to his fish. He hoped to be a taxidermist and was trying to reconstruct the bones of his trout almandine. Sharlie focused on the couple at the door. When the redhead murmured something again, then headed in the direction of the restrooms, Sharlie rose so quickly that she almost upset the table.

"Excuse me, please. I—I'll be right back. I have to use the ladies' room." Confident that her date would watch his trout and not her, Sharlie made no pretense of moving toward the ladies' room, but scuttled immediately to the foyer and to Jared Wright.

Jared's eyes widened in appropriate surprise and even pleasure when he saw her.

"Well, fancy meeting you here!"

"Yesss," Sharlie hissed. "Fancy it."

"How's your date?"

"So good, it's scary." She blew a curl out of her eyes and glared at him. "What are you doing here, Jared? Appearing at the scene of the crime?"

Jared pretended to look puzzled, and Sharlie ached to slug him. "What crime?"

"Christopher Robin," she snarled. "What's the idea? He just spent forty-five minutes explaining the finer points of insect appreciation."

"So? Sounds interesting."

"I was eating my salad. I don't want to know which bugs live on romaine!" Sharlie lost the struggle to keep her voice down. "I just want to know why you did it, Jared. What's the big idea? This is your idea of my dream date?"

"I think you're being a little judgmental," Jared said equably. "You've just met the man."

"*Boy,* Jared, *boy.* What is he, eighteen?"

"Last May," he affirmed pleasantly. "Quite a party from what his parents said."

You cannot kill a man in the foyer of a lovely restaurant, Sharlie told herself grimly. Perhaps she should ask him to step outside. "Who is your date?"

Jared glanced in the direction the lovely redhead had gone and crossed his arms over his chest in a repulsively self-satisfied manner. "Remember you were asking about my evenings?"

"This is what you do with them?"

"Well, no, not every evening. Sometimes we prefer Chinese food. Last week Ruby wanted manicotti, so—"

"Ruby? That's her name?"

"Yep." Jared smiled. "Her parents named her before her hair started coming in. They had no idea she was going to be a redhead. Isn't that amazing?"

"Stunning. Good thing they didn't name her Emerald."

Jared frowned reprovingly. "Her parents are old friends of the family. So is Ruby."

"Old?"

"A friend."

Ruby chose that moment to reappear, and Sharlie was treated to a far better view than she wanted of Ruby's blatant curves sashaying elegantly beneath a shirred front, strapless dress in forest-green satin. Ruby smiled broadly when Jared introduced the two women. She held out a silky hand for Sharlie to shake.

"It's a pleasure to meet you at last. Jared's told me so much about you. I was bursting with curiosity."

Sharlie shot Jared a suspicious look. "There's not that much to tell, really."

Jared put his hands in the pockets of his trousers and shrugged. "I told her that you're a great cook. I told her about all those wonderful meals you've been making for us."

Terrific. Sharlie felt like the Pillsbury Doughboy. No wonder she was with Christopher Robin, and Ruby had Jared. "I'm not only a cook," she felt compelled to inform. "I . . . draw, too."

"Jared told me." Ruby nodded enthusiastically. "I would love to see your work sometime soon. I'm an artist, too. Sculpture and ceramics mostly, but I have some really wonderful watercolors in my gallery. Have Jared bring you by. Or stop by yourself. It's on the main drag, you can't miss it."

Sharlie stared at Ruby. Sexy, talented and her own art gallery, too? This conversation was becoming positively painful. At least the woman could have the decency to be rude or condescending. Sharlie rolled and straightened her shoulders. She didn't have to stand here and listen to this; she could go home and feel insecure.

"Excuse me," she said, her lips curving sweetly at the dynamic duo. "But I had better get back to my date."

Jared nodded, his hands still balled into fists and stuffed in his pockets. There was a grim, brooding expression creeping over his features, but Ruby flashed her lovely smile and said something charming in parting.

Sharlie headed back to the table and to Christopher Robin, who didn't seem to care that she had been gone, and who wasn't exhibiting much interest in her return, either. He was busy studying the skeleton of his trout. Sharlie concentrated on her now cold lamb in order to avoid making eye contact with Jared and Ruby as they were shown to their table. At the first opportunity she pleaded a headache and asked Christopher Robin if they could return to the inn. He was only too happy to oblige. After securing two doggy bags, one for Sharlie's lamb and one for his trout bones, they left the restaurant without further ado.

Back at the inn Sharlie fed lamb to Lotty and furiously beat batter for the next morning's banana crunch cake. When everybody had retired for the evening, she changed into pajamas and a robe, made a mug of hot cocoa and folded herself into a chair in the library.

ᐟ It was nearing midnight and still Jared had not returned. Sharlie had been torturing herself with thoughts of Ruby and Jared all evening. She no longer had to wonder why her friend, her good friend, had seen fit to set her up with a man...a boy...whose idea of fun was examining his fish bones. Next to Ruby he saw her as an inexperienced girl.

On the heels of this realization, however, came another revelation. She had felt not only comfortable with Jared these past several weeks, she had felt womanly, secure, attractive and engaging. She could be herself, and she actually liked that self when she was with Jared. She knew now that a good part of that feeling was derived from her belief that Jared saw her as a woman, and that he liked what he saw as well. If she was mistaken about Jared's perceptions, what would that do to her newfound perception of herself? Would it crumble?

Sharlie took a sip of cocoa. In all honesty, even standing next to Ruby hadn't made her feel unattractive, just a little green around the gills when she saw the other woman's figure.

Sharlie grew ever more thoughtful. She didn't feel less secure than she had before the evening had begun, at least as far as her own worth was concerned. But she was lonely. It was the same feeling she had experienced on a number of occasions when Jared was gone for the evening, but tonight it was more pronounced, more pervasive, because tonight she knew that he was snuggled cozily with someone else.

Deep in the night, when she was alone with her hot chocolate and her flannel robe, it seemed that everyone in the world was part of a pair and that she alone was a single. It was also at times like this that she had begun to wonder of late whether having a fling was the kind of experience she was truly looking for. The idea of starting a relationship just to find out what everybody else knew was starting to seem ... stupid. She wanted to share with someone, to explore all the facets of herself, not to have an affair just so she could feel like somebody else.

What was Jared doing with Ruby right now? Did he want to marry her, or were they too sophisticated for that? Sharlie thought about Jared spending the evening with the beauteous and, no doubt, scintillating Ruby while, thanks to Jared, she was stuck with the taxidermy kid.

The front door opened and closed and Sharlie was up and out of her chair in an instant. She raced out of the library, through the den and into the foyer with her robe flapping about her pajama-clad ankles. Jared stood just inside the door, his jacket off and thrown over his shoulder and his tie loosened. Sharlie crossed her arms and looked at him with a scowl. At least his shirt and tie were still on.

"You took your time coming back!" she blurted.

Jared looked at her in tired surprise. "What are you doing up?" He cocked a brow. "Where's Christopher?"

"Never mind." She pointed a finger at Jared's chest. "From now on I pick out my own dates. You obviously have no desire to help me and no idea of what I'm looking for."

Jared drew his coat down from over his shoulder and sighed. He seemed weary and was not up to a sparring match. "What are you looking for?"

Sharlie pushed at the sleeves of her robe. "You don't have to worry about it. Just remember that from now on, I handle my own life. And if you can't help me out of friendship and a kind regard for the relationship we've developed, then ... just forget it!"

Jared looked at Sharlie soberly. "I do have a great regard for our relationship, Sharlie. And I'm sorry you had such a bad time tonight. Will you let me make it up to you?"

Sharlie shrugged. Hurt. Hurt was what she had been all evening, when she thought that Jared perceived her as a romantic washout. And she felt a churning frustration that the man whose company she enjoyed every minute they were together preferred the company of another woman in the evenings. She looked at him suspiciously.

"How?"

"The Annual End-of-Summer Costume Party is coming up in a couple of weeks. Will you go with me?"

"What Annual End-of-Summer Costume Party?"

"The one we have every year at the end of the summer. Will you go with me?"

"Aren't you going with anyone?"

"I think I'll be going with you, if you'll answer my question. Will you go with me?"

Sharlie had barely been able to contain herself when Jared had walked in the door this evening. The mere thought of spending time with him made her pulse flutter in anticipation. She liked him, and she wanted to go with him. She wanted it entirely too much. For Jared's benefit, she shrugged again.

"I guess."

"Thank you. Your enthusiasm underwhelms me."

"Oh, I'm enthused," Sharlie assured him with a smile. "Particularly as you'll be making this evening up to me."

Jared grinned, some of the guilty tension fading away. "Just leave everything to me. I'll even get our costumes. How do you feel about Bonnie and Clyde?"

"Can I be Clyde?"

Jared frowned. "Porgy and Bess? No? Well, I'll give it some thought. In the meantime, be nice to Christopher Robin." Jared leaned close and whispered, "I think he really liked you."

"You're not funny, Jared," Sharlie snapped. "Christopher Robin paid more attention to his fish skeleton than he did to me, and I told the restaurant to charge the dinner to the inn, because the whole night was your fault. And if you think—"

Jared nodded agreeably as he plodded up the steps with Sharlie hot on his heels, her monologue raining pleasantly around him as he walked. His face was a mask of polite commiseration as he listened, but inside he smiled with pleasure. Sharlie's arms flailed in the quilted flannel robe, which was much too warm for summer. Her hair was a wild, disordered mop of curls, and her face was flushed as she lectured. She was some kind of woman.

The following week brought an interesting development to Sharlie's limp social life. In fact, it brought the life to her social life.

It was Monday afternoon, dull and slow with most of the previous week's guests already on their way home and most of the new arrivals scheduled for later in the week. Jared was back in San Francisco for a meeting with his staff, and Sharlie felt a gnawing frustration as she considered her relatively limited options for the evening ahead.

She was staring at cookie dough, wondering if investing in a variety of cookie cutters might add a perk to her day, when Mrs. Manzer came bustling into the kitchen, her cheeks flushed with excitement.

"I just saw the most handsome man I have ever seen, more handsome than a movie star!" she chirped, her motherly hands clutched to her bosom in ecstasy. "He looks like Clark Gable, only I hear they put makeup on Clark Gable—can you imagine?—and Mr. McLeod isn't wearing any makeup, I'm sure of it." She giggled happily. "I shouldn't get so flustered, a woman of my age talking about a young man like that, but I'll tell you, I'm not too old yet to appreciate beauty. And that is one beautiful man!" She melted onto the oak bar stool, resting her arms on the countertop.

Sharlie pulled a cookie sheet out of the cupboard and started rolling the cookie dough into balls. She liked working to the tune of Mrs. Manzer's chatter. "Who is he?"

"He's Mr. McLeod." Mrs. Manzer plucked a ball of cookie dough from Sharlie's sheet and nibbled with tiny

bites. "And he's here at our inn. I checked him in myself,"
she added with satisfaction. "And on a Monday, too." She
wagged her head in wonder. "He's a stock broker from Los
Angeles, tall, very elegant and suave. He's here to relax, he
says, and he's here alone."

Mrs. Manzer raised her brows as if that statement held
some special significance. "No wedding ring, either. Maybe
he's here to recuperate from a sour love affair. Or poor in-
vestments."

"Did he seem upset?" Sharlie plopped another ball of
dough onto her cookie sheet, and watched as the ball was
plopped into Mrs. Manzer's mouth.

"No," she admitted, "he didn't seem upset. A little tired,
perhaps. I told him that as he missed afternoon tea in the
lounge, I'd bring a pot up to his room. And some of your
muffins and tea cakes, also. I'll just warm them a bit."

She set about making fresh tea and heating the muffins.
"I told him about the costume party next week, but he said
he only planned on staying a week, and then he was going
to go to San Simeon, but I told him San Simeon's not all
that far, you could stay here and go to San Simeon on a day
trip. Here's the best place to relax and find yourself again,
I told him." She laughed merrily. "That was forward
enough, don't you think?"

Sharlie shrugged. "Oh, I don't think he—"

"Oh, you know it was," Mrs. Manzer chortled. "Well, I
don't care. It's seldom enough we get a bachelor that good-
looking, and I don't mind if I do a bit of matchmaking."

Sharlie looked at Mrs. Manzer with a start. Visions of
Clark Gables danced in her head. Mrs. Manzer was a
sweetheart for thinking of her.

Ever since Jared had gone to San Francisco, Sharlie had
tried to explore her feelings for the man. So far she had dis-
covered that she didn't want to think about it. Being friends
with Jared was easy; it was gratifying. She could reach out

in friendship and know with perfect certainty that he would respond. She liked certainty. It was so soothingly definite.

There would be no guarantees with Mr. McLeod of the Clark Gable mug, of course, but that was okay. He could reject her, and she wouldn't crumble. Probably.

In any event, cultivating an interest in Mr. McLeod could take her mind and her emotions off Jared. And that would be a terrific relief. Because if she was so stupid as to actually feel a bit of passion for Jared, then he could reject her, and she would crumble. Definitely. Maybe only temporarily, but definitely. She really didn't want to think about it.

Clark Gable. She would think about that. She had seen *Gone with the Wind* seven times, and that was before it came out on video. Sharlie shaped a piece of dough between her fingers. Plan A for Affair could be back in action with a vengeance. In fact, with a candidate this perfect, Plan B for Beautiful Permanent Union might be worth a thought. She looked at Mrs. Manzer.

"He really looks like Clark Gable?"

"Exactly. Except that he's blond. Really, it's uncanny."

"Hmm." She rolled the ball of dough between her palms. "Did he say anything about taxidermy?"

"What?"

"Never mind. Do you really think he'll stay until the party?"

Mrs. Manzer nodded.

"You really think he's single?"

She nodded excitedly. "Oh, I do hope so. It's about time Ruby found a good man, and this could be the perfect opportunity. They'd make such a beautiful couple, don't you think?"

The little round ball of dough became a flat little heap. "Ruby?"

"Yes. She has a lovely, large house on the water. We always have the costume party there. But it's no good to live in a place that big all by yourself. I bet as soon as he sees her, he'll fall for her. Men always do, and I've known Ruby all her life."

Sharlie stared at Mrs. Manzer's back as the woman set a picturesque afternoon tea on a tray and prepared to carry it upstairs to their new guest.

"I think I've got everything. Does that look like everything?"

Sharlie glanced at the tray. "That's everything."

How could Mrs. Manzer not know about Jared and Ruby? Unless, of course, Sharlie was right, and they were having an illicit, covert, sneaky affair that they weren't proud enough of to bring out into the open. Should Sharlie be the one to enlighten her? She shook her head. Certainly not; it wasn't her place. Besides, she had other fish to fry. There was an eligible bachelor in the house. Sharlie smiled. If the way to Mr. Perfect's heart was through his stomach, then afternoon tea was just the beginning.

Mrs. Manzer hefted the tray into her arms and started out the door, then had a sudden thought that turned her back.

"By the way, what are you making for dinner? He might not want to look for a restaurant on his first night."

Sharlie thought of the chicken, sitting in the refrigerator, waiting to be doused with barbecue sauce.

"Roast loin of pork," she improvised, "au Grand Marnier. and a carrot soufflé. Pomme de terre Dauphin and a bourbon apple tart for dessert."

"On a Monday night?" Mrs. Manzer exclaimed, obviously pleased. "Well, isn't that a stroke of luck."

"Yes, indeed. Uh, dinner won't be served until seven. I'm having a little trouble with the soufflé."

Chapter Nine

Monday's dinner was a smashing triumph, and Tuesday's breakfast—buckwheat blinis and stuffed French toast with sweet raspberry butter—was a hit. The gorgeous H.B. was swooning with pleasure by the time tea rolled through the lounge on Tuesday afternoon, and Sharlie, who had not yet made a personal appearance, was ready to make her move. As soon as the last apricot scone was out of the oven and the cream was whipped, Sharlie rushed upstairs to prepare for part two of Seduce the Hunk.

She dressed with care in a mandarin-style blouse of strawberry-red silk over cream silk trousers. She pulled her hair up in back with a pretty rhinestone clasp and used her makeup to design a face that was regal and composed. Then she breezed downstairs and strolled casually into the lounge to introduce herself as the chef and to serenely inquire whether the tea was to everybody's liking. The expression of sheer surprise and delight on H.B.'s face made the past day's plotting and excessive cooking all worthwhile.

H.B. rose as Sharlie approached, and although she had sneaked several peeks at the man between yesterday evening and this afternoon, she was unprepared for the sheer force of his appearance. He was as tall as Jared and blatantly handsome. His golden hair was thick and shining; his jaw, a sculptor's dream. His eyes sparkled with deep blue intensity, and the flash of his smile made Sharlie want to snap a quick photo. There would be no room for argument in discussing this man's appeal; he was objectively, unarguably a knockout.

Sharlie's hand inched out to meet his, and her fingers were held with tender care.

"I admit to a prejudice," H.B. said. "You've just destroyed my image of Betty Crocker."

H.B.'s eyes, his voice, his entire manner left no doubt that a lavish compliment underscored his words. Sharlie melted into her chair.

For the better part of an hour, they conversed on a variety of topics. The lounge was empty save for the pair of them when the front door opened, and a tumble of voices sounded in the foyer. Sharlie heard footsteps marching up the stairs and Mrs. Manzer's busy voice chattering gaily, and she knew that more guests had arrived. She was debating over whether she should wrench herself away from H.B., when the door to the lounge was filled, and Sharlie glanced up to see Jared. Surprise colored his smile.

H.B. stood. The beam of his grin shot out at Jared as the two men moved toward each other to clasp hands. H.B. gave Jared a hearty clap on the back.

Jared shook his head. "What are you doing here?"

H.B. laughed. "Nice welcome, buddy. Stockbrokers need vacations, too. So, I've decided to take you at your word and see if this inn is the paradise you claim it is." He looked at Sharlie. "So far, you're an honest man."

Sharlie nearly giggled, but managed instead to preserve her hold on her dignity. She peeked over at Jared and felt a distinct sense of satisfaction. His smile had turned swiftly to a frown.

"Is Cynthia with you?"

H.B. grimaced. "That was over a year ago." His gaze again included Sharlie. "And I don't think I should bore us all with the bloody details now." He smiled charmingly. "Especially not when the present company is so good."

Sharlie returned his smile and did not fail to notice the deepening of Jared's frown. She addressed her employer with relish.

"What are you doing back so early in the week, Jared? I didn't expect you for another two days, at least."

"It's not a busy week. I brought some work back with me." It was a lie that his secretary would have called him on. "Besides, I'm supposed to be vacationing," he muttered grimly. He had not relished walking out on his office and then walking in on a glamorized Sharlie talking to H. B. "The Lech" McLeod.

He studied Sharlie discreetly, then offered a mocking look for her alone. "Nice outfit. Special occasion?"

Sharlie quelled him with a glare. "You know I like to dress well when I'm not working." She turned to H.B. and shrugged coquettishly. "It's so hot in that stuffy kitchen. It's such a pleasure to dress up and just be a girl again."

Jared's brows rose in disbelief, but H.B. nodded in sympathy.

Taking Sharlie's arm, Jared guided her toward the door. "If you'll excuse us for just a moment, H.B., there are some things I need to discuss with my chef. I'll bring her back when she turns into a girl again."

Sharlie dug her heels into the Persian rug and refused to budge. Jared gave her a yank.

"Come along, Charlene. You can tell me what you don't like about the kitchen."

Sharlie stomped angrily in front of him until she realized that this would be the perfect time to gloat with complete

freedom over the obvious effect she was having on a man of
H.B.'s caliber. And he was Jared's friend, no less, a truly
delicious bonus. In the kitchen she turned to Jared, and her
cherry-red lips curved ferally.

"Welcome back, Jared. I like your friend."

"Uh-huh. How long has he been here?"

"Why didn't you ask him?"

"I'm asking you," Jared snapped. "He couldn't have
been here more than a day. I've only been gone since Monday."

"He got here Monday afternoon, actually. Why is it so
important? Seems to me that the really important point is
that he's here."

Jared gave a snort of disbelief. "Don't tell me you fell for
his type?"

"What type?" Sharlie scoffed. "He's gorgeous, charming and utterly fascinating. And you know it! The only thing
that's bothering you is that I got him all by myself."

Jared folded his arms over his chest, his warm brown eyes
mocking her freely now. "Is he yours already, Sharlie?"

Sharlie scowled. "It's a figure of speech, but he's definitely attracted . . . and you know it!"

Jared wagged his head. "I don't know any such thing.
H.B. is always smooth with the ladies."

Sharlie felt anger brewing, but willed herself to stay se-
rene. "I've finally figured you out, Jared, so you're not
going to make me angry anymore. You know what your
problem is? You have a madonna-whore complex."

"What?!"

"That's right." Ignoring the fact that her theory was improvised, Sharlie was adamant. "You see me as someone
naive and 'pure,' someone you can talk to and confide in
and be friends with without ever having to even think about
something as complicated as sexuality. That makes everything very simple and relaxing for you, but if I find someone I want to have an affair with, then you have to see me

as other men do—as a woman, and that would complicate matters." She barely paused for a breath. "Then I wouldn't be your little buddy anymore. Not only that, but then you'd realize that there aren't any fairy tales, no Cinderellas left for a prince like you to rescue. You'd be out of a job, Mr. Self-Appointed Hero."

Sharlie folded her arms with complacent satisfaction. She'd read *The Cinderella Complex;* she'd listened to Irene Kassorla. Her psychology was airtight.

Jared's jaw had dropped a bit with every word she spoke. There was a considerable pause as he stared at her. When he spoke, his voice was tight with anger.

"You are insane. How do you come up with this crap?"

"I know what I'm talking about."

"Do you?" Jared was furious. He was as furious and hurt and frustrated as he had ever been in his life. And he wanted to hurt back.

"There's a little loophole in your analysis, Dr. Kincaid. You're assuming that I have to fight off an attraction for you. I don't. If I treat you like a child, it's because that's what you've been since I met you—a child trying to play adult games. Women don't feel compelled to embark on affairs with strangers just to prove to themselves that they are women."

Pain rose from Sharlie's stomach and glittered in her eyes. Immediately she tried to shutter her expression. Until this moment, she had been ignorant of how strongly Jared's opinion mattered to her. Now she felt helpless to hide.

From the moment they met, he had seen through every facade, had meticulously pecked away at every pose. He had uncovered the little girl, the opinionated friend; now he struck to the core of the vulnerable woman who, once again, was looking for love in the wrong place.

Jared did not stay angry long. At the first glimpse of the hurt he had inflicted, his hand came up to touch her shoulder.

"Sharlie, I didn't—"

But Sharlie wanted none of it. She wanted to run—behind any facade, any pose she could get her hands on.

Backing stiffly away, she raised her head and jutted her chin in her best Katherine Hepburn impersonation. It lasted all of one second. Her face crumpled as quickly as it posed.

Her blond curls were an angelic frame around her down-turned face, but her eyes were stormy and as temperamental as the tide. For a moment her lips quivered. She looked as though she were about to say something, but no words came. She turned and walked rapidly to her room.

Jared's eyes followed her up the stairs, but his body stayed behind. Every inch of him was filled with biting frustration.

What was the matter with him? He was a grown man who wanted only to hold and lavish affection on the woman who had been invading his dreams for weeks. Instead he was playing games, trading taunts, acting like a petulant imbecile.

He didn't want Sharlie to be attracted to H.B. It was as simple as that. He needed more time to win her for himself. It was too bad his mother had chosen Northern California for the site of their inn. If they'd been a little more exotic, he could have summoned her to work on a deserted island.

"Well, it's about time you two—"

H.B. stopped mid-sentence and leaned to his right to peer around Jared.

"I don't see Sharlie behind you, do I?" he murmured wryly, taking a substantial sip of the dry sherry he had substituted for tea when left to his own devices.

"No," Jared answered, taking a step into the library and closing the door behind him, "you don't."

H.B. sighed and made himself comfortable in one of the cushioned chairs.

"It's not that I'm not happy to see you again, Jared, but I was enjoying Sharlie's company. Don't suppose you'd care to leave and send her back in, would you?"

"Not really."

H.B. shook his head mournfully. "Ah, and this vacation was beginning to look like my best idea in years."

"It will be your last idea in years if you get cute with Sharlie," Jared warned with cold determination.

"But I'm always cute," H.B. said amiably. "Women tell me so all the time. It's really quite pleasant."

"Yeah." Jared pointed to the tea service resting on the mahogany table. "What kind of tea is it today?"

H.B. waved his sherry glass. "How should I know? You don't expect me to drink that swill, do you? I hate tea. Come to think of it, I'm not thrilled with sherry, either. You're very poorly stocked, if you don't mind my saying so."

Jared shrugged and poured himself a cup of tea. "I might be able to dig up something more to your taste before you leave."

There was a heavily implied *if* at the end of Jared's comment, and H.B. groaned.

"Why am I getting the distinct impression that you are about to ruin my vacation?"

Jared smiled at his friend. "Jasmine."

"What?"

"This is jasmine tea. Sharlie loves it."

H.B. nodded. "Well, that's good to know."

"I know a lot about Sharlie. More, probably, than she would like me to know."

"Oh-oh." H.B. mumbled into his sherry. Jared had warning signs flashing all over him.

"Given the duration of our friendship, and knowing your background as well as I do," Jared began, leaning against the fireplace mantel, "I feel quite comfortable telling you that if you so much as breathe on Sharlie, I will find you and hurt you."

He took a sip of his tea, while H.B. cleared his throat noisily and shifted in his chair.

"I see. Oookay." H.B. held up a hand. "Just one problem, though. It seems that we—Sharlie and I—have this little . . . date."

"When?"

"Tomorrow night."

"Where?"

"I don't know yet. I'm not that familiar with the area. I don't suppose it would do any good to ask you to recommend a quiet little . . . no, I guess not."

Setting his sherry on the coffee table and making a great show of straightening his silk tie, H.B. watched his friend covertly.

"You know, Jared, there may not be a graceful way to break this date. After all, I have no real reason to break it, and there are human feelings involved here. When Sharlie asked me—"

"She asked you?"

H.B. swallowed his grin behind a mask of sheer innocence.

"Yes." He stood and pressed the fingers of one hand to his forehead. His other hand splayed across his hip as he paced. "I hate to reject her so blatantly. I already told her I was perfectly free. Well, I suppose I could tell her I'm not hungry, or something, tomorrow. She might believe that. Of course, you know her better than I."

Jared's fingers tightened around the teacup.

"All right," he growled, "you can go out with her." He put the cup back on the tray and smiled grimly at his friend. "But we're going to establish a few ground rules, first."

"Rules?" H.B. shuddered expressively. "How I hate that word."

Alone in her room, without even her formerly trustworthy feline to comfort her, Sharlie paced moodily.

She had done it again.

She was attracted to the wrong man. H.B., dashing and rather appealing in his own way, had asked her out almost immediately. Had she been excited? Oh, yes. She had been bursting with anticipation—the anticipation of what Jared would do when she told him. Would he look uncomfortable? Relieved? Flat-out jealous? She had been hoping for jealous.

She was crazy about the wrong man.

Jared's reaction to her incipient date with H.B. had infuriated her. His nonchalance was insulting. Faced with the probability that he wasn't jealous, that the image of her evening with his handsome, eligible, eager, male friend moved Jared not at all, Sharlie had felt compelled to goad him into a reaction. When that reaction came, it doused the flickering hope that Jared would admit that he was attracted to her. She was devastated.

She was in love with the wrong man.

Again.

"Oh, no." Sharlie released a miserable groan and fell back on her bed. She covered her eyes with her palms and rolled her head on the quilt. This was worse than before.

Happiness with Glen had been sweet and simple and mostly imagined. When he didn't love her, her misery had stemmed from not realizing the love she had imagined. Happiness with Jared was hilarious and furious and real. Her emotions were wide awake when she was with him, and he was telling her to put them to bed again.

Well, she didn't want to.

A knock sounded on her door.

"It's Jared." His voice was low and tentative. "May I come in for a moment?"

"Just a minute."

She brought her hands down from her face, sat up and straightened her mandarin blouse. She reached up to check her hair.

Composed, she instructed herself. *You will be very composed.* Taking a steadying breath, she went to the door. "Come in."

She stood aside and allowed Jared to enter. He crossed to her window, and they stood staring at each other. For the first time their silence seemed awkward.

Why can't I just say what I feel and have it all work out? Sharlie wondered forlornly. *If honesty is the best policy, then I can speak and be on my honeymoon by Friday.*

Jared felt like a teenager who had sneaked into the girl's dormitory. Sharlie was looking at him, her eyes big and luminous, her little feet in stockings and peeking out from under the Rodeo-Drive pants she was wearing. He was very thankful for those toes. She had obviously gone to a great deal of trouble to look sophisticated tonight, and she had succeeded. At the moment she appeared cool, almost haughty. He took a deep breath. Only her toes looked familiar, as they curled shyly into the floor.

"Sharlie, I just wanted to tell you that...uh, before...I, umm..." He halted ignominiously. One line in, and he was floundering already. It was her face that was throwing him. Usually her features were mobile, a kaleidoscope of emotion. Now she was so damned composed, her face looked like a mask.

"What do you want to tell me?"

"What? Oh—that before, when we were downstairs, I should have told you...I should have said that I...that you...look nice in that color."

Jared smiled. He was thoroughly disgusted with himself, but there was no need for her to know that. He had meant to come up here and tell her that he was jealous of H.B. That he didn't want her for a buddy; he wanted her for his love. But he didn't know how.

Now she was looking at him like he was crazy. *Don't just stand here,* he blasted himself, *say something else.*

"I also wanted to tell you that I'm sorry I said what I did."

Sharlie's features softened a bit. She shook her head. "It was my fault. I never should have—"

"No, no. It was mine. I had no right—"

"Well, true, but if I hadn't said—"

"What does that have to do with it? You had every right."

"No, I didn't. How else could you react?"

"Sharlie, for crying out loud, will you—"

"Please, Jared, let me finish..."

"Let *you* finish? I'm the one who came in here...."

Jared paused, and a slow grin spread across his face and reached out to Sharlie. He shook his head. "I just wanted to say I'm sorry," Jared told her softly.

Sharlie nodded. "So am I. I don't know why I said all that. It's just that you...you're my friend. I suppose I wanted you to be happy for me."

"You're right," Jared acceded sincerely. "And I am."

Coward, Sharlie accused herself silently.

Fool, Jared berated himself.

"So when are you going out with H.B.?"

"Tomorrow."

"That's great."

Sharlie nodded.

"Well." He moved past her and opened the door. "I'd better let you get your beauty sleep."

"Oh. Thanks."

"Feel free to knock off an hour or two early tomorrow. We can cover for you."

"Thank you."

He turned once before he left. "See you tomorrow."

Jared closed the door and walked across the hall to his own room. His mood was grim, to say the least. So Sharlie wanted a date with H.B. and a nod of approval from her "friend" Jared, eh? Well, what was he—chopped liver?

Stripping off his jacket and tie, he threw them onto a chair and crossed into the bathroom. He twisted the shower on full blast and felt some satisfaction as angry steam rose to the ceiling.

All right, he thought, all right. There was more than one way to win a war.

In her room Sharlie moved toward the window. She stopped and stood in the spot Jared had just vacated. Somehow, whenever he left a room, she didn't feel alone. It was as if he left his presence with her.

Sighing, she lowered herself onto the window seat. She and Jared were friends again.

"Yippee."

Wondering about Jared's abrupt about-face regarding her date with H.B., Sharlie leaned on the windowsill. There was a romantic slice of moon resting high in the dark sky tonight. Delicate wisps of clouds wove around the stars. Tomorrow night she might be standing under the moon with H.B. What would Jared say then? "That's great"?

No! Sharlie smacked her hand on the window seat. She would not give up without a fight. There had to be some way to reach Jared, or to determine once and for all time that there was no hope, not a shred, not an ounce. Until then she would have to regroup and find a new strategy.

The battle isn't over yet, she vowed, not by a long shot.

Chapter Ten

Candlelight played over Sharlie's hair, flickering gently across her face and down her neck. The golden light cast a lovely glow on the entire evening.

The effect was not wasted on H.B.

"I picked a perfect restaurant," he congratulated himself amiably, leaning over the table toward his date. "Always insist on candlelight."

Sharlie smiled and fiddled with her napkin. "I will."

"You look lovely in peach."

"Thank you."

H.B. rested his chin in his hand and beamed. "You're not used to flattery." He wagged his head. "What happened to Jared to make him such a scrooge with compliments?"

Sharlie had already gleaned two important bits of information about H.B.: one, he never asked a question when he could make a statement; and two, most of his questions were either rhetorical or tongue-in-cheek, anyway. Wisely, she said nothing.

"I almost vacationed in Hawaii this year," H.B. continued. "Palm trees and pineapples have never held less appeal."

His voice was a silky purr, but Sharlie heard the humor
behind it. He was playing a parody of himself. Her eyes
sparkled.

"What about girls in grass skirts?"

"I'm allergic to grass."

Sharlie laughed for the first time that evening.

"Now tell me." H.B.'s blue eyes were sharp and direct.
"What's a clever girl like you doing in a quaint little inn?"

Sharlie looked up from her zabaglione. H.B. colored the
word *quaint* as though its very definition were *yucky*.

"I thought you liked the inn." She pointed a pink-
polished finger. "You told Jared that the inn is 'charming.'
I heard you."

"It is charming. But you're cosmopolitan. You're city."

Sharlie shook her head. "No, it's just my hair. It's supposed to make you think that."

H.B. laughed heartily. "You see? You are a treasure."

Looking at H.B. and noting the way his eyes twinkled
with delight, Sharlie couldn't help but imagine Jared sitting in H.B.'s place. At the moment, she felt relaxed and
slightly amused. With Jared across from her, the candles
glowing moodily between them, the amusement would fade
and passion would rise to the forefront.

Realizing that she was about to spend an evening pictur-
ing Jared's head on H.B.'s neck, she tried to snap out of it
and focus on her dinner companion. She searched her meager repertoire for suitable small talk.

"Have you known Jared long?"

While H.B. leaned back and gazed at Sharlie, she played
with her spoon and hated herself for hoping that he
wouldn't change the topic.

"I've known him since college," H.B. said. "We were
fraternity brothers."

"Jared—you and Jared belonged to a fraternity?"

"Well, of course. What else were two eligible, great looking, potentially successful young sophomores to do? Actually, Jared had to be dragged." H.B. looked disgusted. "He never knew what was good for him."

"Did you like it?"

"I did. Jared left before the end of his junior year. He didn't like the discrimination."

When Sharlie's brows rose, H.B. smiled. "Not racial discrimination or religious. But we were one of the 'good' fraternities, if you know what I mean. There were certain qualifications."

Sharlie nodded. "You mean you were popular with the sororities."

H.B. grinned. "You could say that. Jared was certainly popular with them."

"Really?" She was about to stop enjoying this conversation.

"With one in particular. Their president and Jared were quite a twosome." H.B. reminisced, picking up his coffee cup and relaxing back in his chair again. "Tori Phelpps. She was president of the sorority, secretary of the Spring Fair committee. Beautiful. Tall. Amazing legs. I think she was on the tennis team. She had the shiniest black hair...."

All over her amazing legs, I hope. Sharlie listened grimly as H.B. made the girl sound like a cross between Dorothy Lamour and the Incredible Isis. The description went on ad nauseam.

"Why did they break up?"

"She kept pressuring Jared to rejoin the fraternity. At the very least, she wanted him to attend all the social functions."

"Well, if he was her boyfriend, then he should have." Sharlie snapped. She was not about to be forgiving of a man who had the bad taste to date a walking fantasy. "If you care about someone, then sometimes you have to extend yourself.''

"I think the point was that she didn't care for Jared."

"What do you mean? Why not?"

"Tori was dedicated to maintaining the proper image. She didn't appreciate Jared's abdication of his fraternity throne.''

"Oh." Sharlie was reasonably contrite. "That's too bad. Was he very hurt?''

H.B. shrugged. "Not as much as he would have been if he'd really loved her. That's my perception, at any rate. And I'm very perceptive.''

He returned his cup to the saucer and leaned both elbows on the table. "How long have you known Jared?"

"Me? Oh, a few months, I suppose. I know his brother-in-law.''

"That's right! Little Gina, married and safe from the likes of me. I haven't seen her in years. I wanted to show her my collection of Proust, which happened to be in the Bahamas at the time.'' Ever glib, H.B. carried on merrily. "Unfortunately, Jared put his foot down.''

"He takes his big-brother role very seriously," Sharlie confirmed morosely.

"He's protective of you, too?" When Sharlie mumbled something affirmative, H.B. was all sympathy. "He's always been hyper-responsible. It's bothersome, isn't it?''

"Sometimes I'd like to kill him.''

H.B. nodded, then clucked disapprovingly. "I hate to betray my gender, but if you ask me, it's the old double standard.''

Sharlie slapped her spoon into the zabaglione. "It is. He feels free to have as many affairs as he wants.'' She shook the spoon at H.B. "And with as many different women as he wants! I mean, I don't know how many women he's stringing along right now, but I bet it's plenty.'' She leaned in and spoke confidentially. "You know, he's rarely home before midnight."

"But expects you to be tucked into bed by nine."

"He expects me to be asexual."

H.B.'s sudden, throaty laughter made heads turn around the room. "Does Jared know you feel this way?"

"No, of course not." Sharlie said. "I mentioned it to him once. He didn't like it."

"I can imagine." H.B.'s cheeks looked like they were about to split from smiling. The knowing look in his eyes became disconcerting.

"You really like Jared, don't you?"

Sharlie grimaced. "Certainly I like him. He's a good friend," she bluffed. She was about to retract everything she had said so far this evening.

Why had she felt the need to fish for information? Why couldn't she simply walk up to Jared and say, "Jared, I know that thus far in our acquaintanceship we've been strictly platonic, but how would you like to have an affair?"

H.B. motioned the waiter to pour more coffee. Hoping that she could cut the evening short, Sharlie started to protest, but H.B. was watching her with a knowing gleam in his eyes.

"Now," he said, rolling his empty sugar packets into balls and tossing them jauntily into the ashtray, "tell your Uncle Hank all about it."

" 'Hank'?"

"I've told only you," he said, grinning. "Come on, now. I have a very bendable ear. And, to be honest, if it's Jared you're interested in, I'd like to see you get him. I think you're just what he needs in his life."

"You do?" Sharlie frowned. "I thought I was supposed to be your date."

H.B. chuckled. "Sharlie, if I thought I had a chance . . ." He let the comment dangle. "So, why haven't you and Jared declared yourselves before now? You've had more than enough time," he admonished, wagging a mocking finger at her.

Sharlie sighed. "Jared's not interested in anything other than friendship," she said, a blasé shrug tagging her words. "And I'm not sure I am, either."

"I see." H.B. tapped his fingertips together and smiled enigmatically. "What if there was a way to find out whether he is interested in something more—and I think that if given the proper nudge he might be—would you want to explore the possibilities in that case?"

Sharlie couldn't help herself. She snapped at the bait like a starved marlon.

"What do you have in mind? It's nothing obvious, is it?" She lowered her delicately plucked brows skeptically. "What makes you think he's interested in me, anyway? He's never given me that impression."

Signaling for the check, H.B. grinned enigmatically. "Patience, Sharlie," he stated calmly. "Patience and trust, and I guarantee that you'll look back on this as a most rewarding endeavor."

A scant hour later, Sharlie and H.B. entered the foyer of the inn to find Jared lounging casually in the living area with a worn book in his hands. He was dressed in heavy brown corduroys and a cream V-neck pullover. Sharlie's eyes went straight to his chest. Jared smiled pleasantly when the couple entered.

"Well, you're back earlier than I expected. Have a nice time?" He rose and crossed the few feet to the foyer as Sharlie and H.B. moved in.

H.B.'s hand was on the small of Sharlie's back, and when she felt a deft nudge, she knew that was her cue to leap into action. She focused her attention on Jared's face and plastered a huge smile across her lips.

"Oh, we had a wonderful time, just wonderful," she enthused, beaming at Jared and darting a flirtatious glance back at H.B. "I had no idea that dancing could be so...creative." As they had planned, she took H.B.'s hand and squeezed it conspicuously.

Jared's welcoming smile slid into a frown as he stared malevolently at the clasped hands of Sharlie and his old school chum. "Creative dancing?" He looked pointedly at H.B. "You went dancing?"

H.B. gave him an innocent shrug over the top of Sharlie's head. "Sharlie said she hadn't gone dancing all summer. Seems a shame with the Itchy Foot so close." He named a popular pub and dance club and asked Jared guilelessly, "Have you been there this summer, Jared?"

Jared's fingers tightened around his book as he stared at H.B.'s neck. "Once," he answered tightly, now openly glaring at his friend.

Sharlie's fingers were twitching, too, but with the urge to grab the book and smack Jared over the head with it. So, he'd been to the Itchy Foot, flirting, no doubt, until his eyeballs had fallen out of their sockets, while she stood alone and tired on a cold kitchen floor, beating popover batter for his mother's afternoon teas. He had never once asked her if she wanted to go dancing. He only took her to libraries and softball fields. Who had he taken to the Itchy Foot—and why hadn't he mentioned it to her if they were supposed to be such great friends? Maybe he thought she didn't know what dancing was. He probably saved adult forms of recreation for long-legged brunette bimbettes, like the one H.B. told her about.

"Where are your glasses?" Jared queried suddenly, staring into her face.

"I'm wearing my contacts," Sharlie told him, her voice chilly.

"She can't see anything without her glasses," Jared informed H.B. confidentially.

"I have contact lenses on," Sharlie repeated tightly.

"We were picnicking on the beach once," Jared said, "she took off her glasses, almost rubbed my back with macaroni salad."

"I'm wearing my contact lenses, dammit!" Both men looked at her in surprise. H.B.'s surprise was laced with delicious amusement.

Jared cocked his head and considered her. "Your eyes are getting puffy."

Sharlie's freshly manicured fingers curled into fists. It gave her some relief to imagine one of those fists making contact with Jared's jaw.

She turned to H.B. "Let's go into the library. We can talk there. I'll make some coffee." She motioned H.B. past her and brushed by Jared without a glance.

He put a hand on her arm. "Aren't I invited for coffee?" he whispered.

"No!" Sharlie hissed at him. "For your information, it was potato salad, and next time it won't be an accident."

When Sharlie left the library some moments later, Jared slipped inside the room and quietly closed the door. He faced H.B., who was lounging in the chair behind the desk, and came right to the point.

"What the hell do you think you're doing?"

H.B. swung his feet off Jared's desk and sat up in the leather chair. "I'm waiting for Sharlie to come back with the coffee."

"Knock it off." Jared strode into the room, his breath coming in exasperated puffs that told H.B. he was in no mood for games. "Why did you take her dancing? You were supposed to have a short, dull dinner and then bring her right back to the inn." Jared emphasized the word *dull* and shot H.B. an accusing look that pinned him to the chair.

H.B. put his hands up in surrender. "It started out dull, I swear. Would I deliberately set out to seduce the girl of

your dreams?'' H.B. asked his friend earnestly. "Of course
not,'' he answered himself, then lowered his head and swung
it slowly from side to side, presenting a lovely picture of a
man consumed with guilt. "She's a beautiful girl, Jared.
And it was her idea to go dancing.'' He smiled fondly.
"She's very affectionate. Not that I couldn't have said no. I
take full responsibility.''

"Responsibility for what?'' Jared bellowed, lunging
across the desk at his supposed friend.

H.B. hopped up and out of harm's way. "For the dancing, the dancing! Really, Jared, you insult me. When a
friend tells me that it's hands off, I respect that.''

H.B. smoothed his tie and looked properly offended. For
a grown man Jared was acting in a deliciously juvenile
manner. And now that H.B. knew that Sharlie was wild
about Jared, but that she, too, refused to admit it—oh, the
comic possibilities were endless.

He stepped out from behind the desk, making a careful
circle around his steaming friend. "On the other hand," he
mused, "if you don't intend to come forward with your
feelings—''

"I do intend to," Jared interrupted firmly. "Just save
whatever you were about to say. As far as you're concerned, Sharlie is a friend only. Understand? Just think of
her as a kid sister...or a nun. Even if I weren't interested,
you aren't right for her.''

H.B. huffed defensively. "She didn't seem to find me too
offensive, but I imagine you're prejudiced." He plopped his
long frame into the chair by the fireplace and put his feet up
on the ottoman. "Now, suppose you tell Uncle Hank your
plan.''

Jared stuffed his fists in his pockets. "Suppose I tell Uncle Hank to take a flying leap," he grumbled. "I didn't
know your name is Hank.''

"I wouldn't tell anyone but you. Now stop being so
squeamish and tell me what you plan to do. I've been known

to give very good advice. Particularly about *une affaire du coeur*."

Jared grimaced, unconvinced, but for the first time in his life, he didn't feel confident enough to go it alone. As well as he thought he knew Sharlie, certain mysteries still remained. The biggest mystery may have been his own reluctance to be straightforward, but he didn't consider that yet. He wondered, instead, why Sharlie was so eager to have a romance with anyone, it seemed, but him.

Jared's full brows came together like thunderclouds. He hated to ask, but his own ego compelled him: "How interested in you is she?"

H.B. lowered his head. He gave every impression of giving the question a great deal of thought, but he was fully aware that the longer he waited, the more agitated Jared grew. When Jared demanded, "Well?" H.B. looked up, thoughtful concern etched deliberately across his face.

"She wants me, Jared." He pressed the tips of his fingertips together to form a steeple and gazed at Jared over the top. "Really, I'm surprised at you. A nice grown-up Lothario like you, afraid to tell a sweet young innocent that you're in love with her."

"I'm *attracted* to her, dammit!" Jared yelled, then lowered his voice. "And it's not a question of being afraid to tell her," he rationalized, finding refuge, as usual, in logic. "It's a question of not wanting to scare her off. She's not too experienced, and right now she thinks of me as her friend. I don't want to jeopardize that or pressure her."

"You're so thoughtful." H.B. beamed approvingly. "Now, if you want my advice, I do believe I have the answer to your dilemma."

Jared hesitated. He didn't want to appear too eager. "What is it?" he grumbled.

"You'll have to trust me," H.B. warned. "I have a great deal of experience in this area, if I do say so myself. First of all, I have to tell you that you are correct—Sharlie thinks of you as a friend only. To her, you are a big brother, Jared, someone to go to for a chat or for advice." H.B. colored the truth mercilessly. He watched gleefully as Jared grew more and more annoyed with each passing syllable. "You're a buddy, a pal, a male Dear Abby, a eunuch—"

"All right!" Jared couldn't take much more. He was beginning to feel like a gelding. "So, what should I do?"

"Change your image," H.B. stated simply. "Make her see you as a man, as a romantic possibility to be reckoned with. She has to see you the way other women see you." H.B. paused then, a worried frown wrinkling his brow. "Other women do see you that way, don't they?"

"Once or twice since high school," Jared growled sarcastically. "And if you're talking about making her jealous, I've already tried that, Dr. Ruth."

"Dr. Ruth would never suggest such a thing," H.B. dismissed. "I, however, know better. You must not have done it properly."

Jared balked, explaining his evening at the restaurant with Ruby and how they had "bumped into" Sharlie and Christopher Robin.

"Pitiful," H.B. declared. "No technique, no style. Of course she was unimpressed. This time you'll listen to me, follow instructions very carefully, and—if you don't mess it up—I guarantee your success."

H.B. leaned back in the chair, his arms crossed behind his head. "Now get out of here before Sharlie gets back."

Jared started to protest, then swallowed his pride and admitted defeat. He needed help with Sharlie. Her contract with the inn would be up in a couple of weeks, and who knew where she'd try to find her "life experiences" then?

He would go to whatever lengths necessary in order to convince Sharlie that he could provide all the romance a girl would require from one lifetime.

"All right, I'm leaving—for now," Jared relented. "But I'll be back as soon as Sharlie goes up to bed," he leaned in and issued his warning, "which had better be soon, and which is definitely going to be alone."

H.B. put his hand to his heart. "Once again, you insult me. We are trying to help you here. That is my chief objective, even though I am on vacation. Now get out," he ordered pleasantly. The curve of his mouth grew wider and wider as he watched Jared's broad back pass through the double doors.

Human Silly Putty.

Gleefully H.B. popped the crystal cork off the sherry decanter and started to pour himself a glass. He remembered that Sharlie was bringing coffee, paused for just a moment, then shrugged and kept pouring. Just a small glass was in order. He had played many a joke in his day; he'd played a joke practically every day in college, but old rock-solid Jared had never allowed himself to be the brunt of a single one. Yet now—H.B. rolled the crystal glass between his fingers and chortled happily—now Jared was a hunk of Homo sapiens clay in H.B.'s hands. And H.B. could bend him any way he wished.

He tossed back the rest of the sherry and set the glass down. His expression became one of happy indulgence. They really were a cute couple, a little juvenile in their approach to romance, but very cute. He wondered—briefly—if it was decent to play with their vulnerable young hearts, then balked at his own hesitation. Of course it was all right. Without his interference . . . or, rather, help . . . they would probably dance around each other, pretending they were strictly friends until they were too tired to be anything else. He would help them—eventually—to discover the truth and each other. And if he had a little fun along the way, well, they'd be too busy thanking him to hold a grudge. In fact, they'd probably look back and laugh just as hard as he planned to. Who knew? He might even cop best man honors at their wedding.

* * *

Sharlie let the soft light from the lamp on the dressing table lull her into a state of placid contemplation. Tucking her legs up beneath her on the window seat and dragging her thin nightgown down over her toes, Sharlie stared out at the moon. It looked properly romantic, full and glowing white in the dark, dark sky.

H.B.'s advice was still ringing in her ears.

"Make Jared see you as a woman, as a romantic force to be reckoned with."

"I tried that," she'd told H.B. "The force wasn't with me."

"You haven't tried it my way. Trust me. Jared will be a goner."

Now Sharlie had to decide if it was worth it. Trying to make a man jealous by using his own good, albeit eager friend as the bait seemed a little low. Also a little intriguing, she smiled, something to tell the grandkids, assuming that Jared ever got around to asking her for a first date.

She sighed. A low thump sounded at her door, and Sharlie glanced at the clock in surprise. One thirty-five a.m. Grabbing her robe, she threw it over her nightgown and crept to the door. The wood floor was cold under her bare feet.

"Yes?" She half-whispered the word, wondering if she had only imagined the knocking.

"Sharlie? I saw the light under your door." Jared's rich voice came to her softly through the oak panel. There was a moment of hesitation on his side and on her own. "May I come in for a minute?"

Sharlie's heart started thumping enthusiastically. She looked down at her nightgown and old robe. Her toes peeked out from beneath the flounce of her pink cotton gown, and she felt stupidly relieved that at least her pink-polished toenails matched her attire.

Jared had seen her in her robe a number of times in the past couple of weeks. He had been making a habit of coming in and relaxing with her for a few moments before he turned in for the night.

At least, she assumed that Jared found their time together relaxing; she found it exhilarating. It provided an intimacy unlike any she had known with a man. Her talks with Glen had never been as naturally companionable or as thrilling as were the moments she spent with Jared in her little room.

So, it was silly to feel shy and giddy now. The new confidence she felt around members of the other gender was a direct outgrowth of the sense of security Jared had helped her find this summer.

Looking back, she wondered if he had deliberately set about boosting her confidence or if her burgeoning self-esteem simply had been a natural by-product of their growing friendship. Did it matter? She opened the door.

Her heart flipped over.

He was still Jared, the same old Jared she'd had no trouble arguing with or scoffing at or crying to for weeks, yet as she looked at him now, her throat constricted. She felt too nervous to say "hello." She could no longer think of him solely as Jared, her friend. What filled her mind now were thoughts of that chest, so warm and broad, snuggled against her in the night. She had the crazy urge to turn off the lights, just so she could hear him speak to her in the dark.

Jared smiled a little, said "Thanks" and walked past her into the room. He stood by the window and looked out at the night.

Seeing her in her nightgown made him want to swoop her up in his arms and deposit her squarely in the middle of the old four-poster, not an original or highly cultivated reaction, Jared thought self-mockingly, but a darn honest one. He would have the same reaction when he was ninety and she was eight-two and still wearing pink cotton to bed.

For weeks he'd been coming in here, chatting about nothing, stalling for time, loving the moments he spent with her in her room. He even loved the tension those moments created, though he'd been taking a considerable number of midnight ocean dips.

There was so much he wanted to say to her. He wanted to take her in his arms and tell her that he was going to be the man to show her the full, romantic love she yearned for.

But there was so much to consider. She was vulnerable, ready to rush into life. He was wiser, more experienced. He owed it to her to wait until she knew what she wanted. He intended to look out for her welfare. He had to be patient, dammit. Didn't he? Dammit, didn't he?

His hands clenched into fists at his side. She had considered every man but him.

He was forced to put more faith into H.B.'s plan than he would have liked, but if it worked and she came to him . . . Oh, he was a desperate man.

Frustration filled his soul. Logic, the companion he'd trusted like a brother, was deserting him now in his hour of need. The very fact that he was here, standing in this room, was proof of how elementary his attraction for her had become. The light under her door had been as potent as a siren's call; he moved like a somnambulist toward her company.

Resigning himself to the circumstances, he turned to engage Sharlie in the nonthreatening conversation he had become such an expert at of late.

"Were you getting ready for bed? Am I keeping you up?"

Jared seemed preoccupied, almost moody, but Sharlie's heart filled with love for him. This time it wasn't a crush. It wasn't infatuation. She loved this man. She loved his humor; but his smugness infuriated her. She loved the way his lower lip rose when he was about to say something logical; but his brotherly concern was killing her. She loved a man, not an idea. She wouldn't forfeit a moment's time with him, even if she were ready to fall asleep standing up.

She shook her head slowly. "I was just sitting, thinking."

"It's hard to go to sleep after a good date," Jared mused aloud. "You tend to stay up, mulling it over." He scowled. Here he was, reduced to fishing for information about another man's date, but at least he could do it subtly.

"Especially if it's a really good date. Then you definitely can't sleep."

He dropped his head. Terrific. That was subtle, all right. Maybe he could ask her to fill out a questionnaire. Disgust crawled across his face.

Sharlie started to demur. *If you want Jared to see you as a woman, make him jealous.* H.B.'s advice dripped through her consciousness like Chinese water torture. *Frustrate him,* H.B. said. *Give him a challenge.*

It seemed devious and wily and sophomoric, but nothing else had worked. She was leaving in three weeks, and she wasn't about to just walk away this time, heart full of yearning, arms as empty as before. She plastered a dreamy smile on her face and nodded.

"Yes, a good date is hard to forget. You just want it to go on and on, especially when he's right here under the same roof." She rolled her eyes and shivered with excitement. "You just want it to go on and on and on and—"

"Yeah, okay, I know!" Jared tried not to gag. "So you think it's the real thing, then?"

Sharlie wasn't sure how to answer that. She wanted Jared to enter the play, not to call it a game and declare H.B. the winner.

"The 'real thing.' What a way to put it," she said. "It's hard to say if it's the 'real thing.' If you mean real love, that is. But I know that I like him enough to see him a great deal. And he lives in Los Angeles. He said we'd be able to see each other quite often and that he'd like to show me his penthouse in Marina del Rey. The bedroom has a picture window overlooking the marina. I've never been in a penthouse."

Sharlie let the thrill of anticipation flood her voice. She looked at Jared for friendly advice. "I think you were right, though, when you said I should go slowly in relationships."

Jared's voice was tight. "Was I?"

"Yes," Sharlie affirmed staunchly. "I would never just move in with H.B."

"That's good." His fist clenched. He shoved it behind his back. "Has he asked you?"

Sharlie wavered. "Not in so many words. But I am a woman, Jared. I can see where we're headed. Personally, I wouldn't mind a weekend commitment."

"A weekend commitment?"

"Yes, you know, see each other on the weekends, most weekends, I should think, but live our own lives on the other days."

"Where would you see each other? In the penthouse with the picture window?"

Sharlie laughed brightly. Now that she was following H.B.'s plan, even using some of the words he'd suggested, she appeared to be making some headway. Jared actually looked a tad jealous.

"Oh, Jared, you're such a stuffy old bear," she teased deliberately, as per part two of H.B.'s Plan: *Convince him that you see him as a friend only and he will go crazy with the desire to be much, much more.*

She fiddled with the sash of her robe and looked up, sweet gratitude fluttering in her eyes and around her smiling lips. "You're so protective of me. I feel like I've had a big brother to watch out for me all summer."

Sharlie got up and crossed to him. She leaned toward him and moved her face close to his cheek. Even as her lips touched his cheek in a kiss that was meant to imply pure sisterly affection, she wondered if she could have got away with planting a sisterly peck on his lips instead.

Jared's cheek was warm and rough and soft. His whiskers, dark even against his tan, were tickling her, and the dark, dark locks of his hair waved within her view. Suddenly the contact between lips and skin was more powerful than Sharlie had ever imagined it could be.

If her will alone could move a man, Jared would turn to her now until their contact became more direct—lips on lips—and the passion and tension mounting in her body would find release in the pressure of their mouths. The scent of his skin made her dizzy.

"I'd better let you get some rest." Jared stood and walked swiftly to the door.

He paused briefly at the threshold and turned to give her a nod. "Good night." He closed the door behind him.

Sharlie remained rooted to her spot by the bed. Wonderful. She hoped H.B.'s plan called for a lot of cold showers, because she was going to need them.

Jared pulled his sweater over his head, rolled it into a ball and hurled it toward his bed. He looked into the mirror and flexed a muscle, just to be sure he still had one.

Her "big brother," huh? Well, wouldn't that be a comfort in his dotage, a condition he felt must be rapidly approaching. He was disgusted with himself. When had it ever been this hard to begin a relationship? When had it ever seemed so impossible to find out where he stood with a woman? Answer: never. Then again, when had the stakes ever been this high? Answer: he didn't want to think about it.

He had always been a risk taker, a man of action. He didn't believe in fearing either rejection or failure; those temporary conditions were just streets you crossed to reach your destination.

But that was before his heart got involved in the whole sticky process. Always before it had seemed to Jared that when one path appeared to be closed, another would open and could be taken instead. Now the only path he wanted was the one that led to Sharlie, and his stride didn't feel as sure as it always had. He kept tripping on his heart.

His mother's words did their maternal duty; they came back to haunt him.

"Try not to let things run *too* smoothly," she'd said. Okay, so he liked control. Who didn't? He knew he tried to maneuver situations—and people. He remembered the pain his mother and sister had suffered when his father had left. Jared had taken up his position as their shelter, their shield, ever since.

What he hadn't realized, what Julia had tried to tell him on numerous occasions, was that he'd been protecting himself, as well, and that he'd been doing too good a job of it. He took care of things. He took care of people. He rarely opened his life to them.

Jared stood there a long time, facing himself and facing his feelings. And finally he saw the truth.

"Admit it," he accused the reflection in the mirror. "You're scared. You're afraid the woman you love might turn you down cold."

Well, damn. There was only one respectable way to handle the problem. He would have to be forthright, to tell Sharlie how he felt and to pray that some responding chord would be struck in her. Even a little responding chord. That was the honorable thing to do, the manly thing.

Jared acknowledged the validity of that sentiment. He acknowledged the rightness of that action. And then he decided to do it H.B.'s way. After Sharlie showed unmistakable signs of interest, there would be time enough to be manly.

But come hell or high water, he would win his woman.

Chapter Eleven

Sharlie was mad. Not angry, not peeved, not righteously indignant. She was mad. Like a crazy dog.

"Don't stop so suddenly!" she hissed at the man ahead of her. "You're making me trip."

"Sorry," Jared hissed back, then sighed. "Try to have a little patience, will you? We'll get the hang of it, if we just work together."

"I don't want to work together. I want to get out of here!" Sharlie bellowed as much as one could bellow while stuffed into the back end of a unicorn costume.

She stamped her hoof.

"Settle down," Jared whispered. "People are beginning to stare at you."

"How do you know they're staring at me?"

"They keep looking behind me."

"Well, I wouldn't know about that, since I can't see anything, now can I?" she growled ferociously. Thoughts of romance fled so swiftly when the man you loved presented you with two hooves and a tail for a costume party. "I want to be up front. Now!"

"I have to be up front, Sharlie," Jared explained again, patiently. "I'm taller, and this head is very heavy. I think the horn is made out of steel."

"You're so considerate," Sharlie intoned dryly. "I'm thirsty. How am I going to get anything to drink back here?"

"I'll head us over to the punch bowl."

Jared started moving, and a second or two later he felt Sharlie stumble after him.

As their hooves moved with a distinct lack of rhythm, Jared kept his unicorn's eyes trained on the crowd of costumed people filling the room. Wherever H.B. was, Jared would find him and stampede him.

In another time and in other circumstances, Jared might have laughed at Sharlie's expression when she realized she was going to the party dressed as a unicorn's hind quarters.

Tonight it hadn't been funny. Jared had bided his time all week, gritting his teeth when Sharlie and H.B. went to the movies, chewing his knuckles when they took their twilight strolls down the beach.

Upon their return Jared would follow H.B.'s instructions, pretending to prepare for a wild evening out. He would don an evening suit or sport jacket and casual shirt. He would pat on the after-shave and whistle a carefree tune as he conspicuously left the inn, whereupon he would head alone to a burger stand. Occasionally he would splurge and take in a movie. Twice, Ruby had taken pity on him, and they played gin rummy until a suitable amount of time had elapsed and Jared thought it was safe to go home.

Every night he tried to keep himself from paying his customary visit to Sharlie, if only to preserve what little was left of his self-respect. He worked out, he read books, he tried to go to sleep early; it never worked. Every night, he was there, knocking on her door, sitting on his pride while

Sharlie regaled him with the juicy details of her outings with H.B.

Jared, in his turn, entertained Sharlie with fictional accounts of unidentified ladies he was supposedly escorting. Then Jared would say good-night, find H.B. and complain loudly that H.B.'s plan stank.

Looking forward to being with Sharlie at the costume party had, at least, kept him going.

But then Jared, trusting desperate soul that he was, had committed himself to H.B.'s "plan" tonight, too. He'd even agreed to let H.B. pick the costume. And where had it landed him? He was stuck in a unicorn head whose cavernous interior must have been nearing a hundred degrees.

Behind him, Sharlie's temper was flaring even higher. She kept kicking him in the fetlock.

"Are you kicking me deliberately?" Jared grumbled tightly to the woman walking in an undignified stoop behind him.

Sharlie snarled at his back. "You got the end with the brain. What do you think?"

"Well, cut it out."

"Just get us to the punch bowl. What's taking you so long?"

"I'm navigating as well as I can," Jared defended himself. "Your end of the costume isn't exactly easy to maneuver. The rear end is actually pretty large—"

"Just watch it," Sharlie warned dangerously. "It's no bigger than your fat unicorn head."

"Nonetheless, I have to move gingerly. It's getting pretty crowded out there."

"It's getting pretty crowded in here, too. I'm about ready to collapse from dehydration."

"Can't have that," Jared said equably. A woman dressed as a mouse skittered in front of him. He tipped his horn to her. "Oh, excuse me. There are a lot of mice costumes here," he told his better half. Sharlie just grunted. "Seems to be a strong animal motif this year,'' he said as he caught sight of a turtle, and then a giraffe who was having trouble holding up his neck.

"It must be my lucky summer," Sharlie remarked unenthusiastically. "What are you doing next year, appliances?"

Jared chuckled. "That reminds me. Once we get to the punch bowl, you're going to have a hard time drinking anything in this costume. Which leads me to an interesting conclusion," he said, beginning to enjoy himself. "You can lead a unicorn to water, but you can't make her—ow!''

Sharlie's hoof made firm contact with the back of Jared's knee. Jared swore.

"Sorry," Sharlie said in a pleasant clip. She was about to add that he deserved it, when a chorus of two feminine voices called out.

"Jared!''

"That is you in there, isn't it?" Voice number two was as deep and sultry as the other tone was high and breezy.

"It's me," she heard Jared acknowledge. "What tipped you off?"

They lowered their voices, and Sharlie strained to listen, but all she caught was voice number two saying something about the unicorn's horn, followed by combined masculine and feminine laughter.

In another second, she was going to buck. All week long she had worked hard to keep from going crazy while H.B. dragged her off to go for walks or to movies whose plots she couldn't remember. She had to keep from screaming or throwing in the towel on H.B.'s plan or doing both every time Jared gussied up and tripped gaily off on one of his dates.

He still came to talk to her at night, but now his conversation was littered with drivel about some woman who had apparently been going to great lengths to entertain him this week. They had driven along the beach in her convertible, had candlelit meals at her place, and one night they had even eaten dinner on an inflatable raft in her pool.

The gory details were enough to put Sharlie off her own food for a week. Looking back, she was shocked that Jared had bothered to come home at all, or that he had managed to come home so relatively early most evenings.

He hadn't revealed the woman's identity, and he had, in fact, indicated that there was more than one woman occupying his time. Still, Sharlie was fairly certain that Ruby, The Redheaded Wonder, must be part of his heavy social calendar.

H.B. kept telling her that everything was working out beautifully. She kept telling H.B. that he was nuts. The moment she had looked forward to all week—attending this party with Jared—was turning into a thoroughly infuriating experience. When she agreed to let Jared pick out the costume, she had expected a little something from *Antony and Cleopatra*. She hadn't expected a lesson in animal husbandry.

She wondered if one of the women talking to Jared now had also found a place in his schedule. She couldn't hear anything in this stupid costume. Sharlie strained as voice number one spoke in her high, flirtatious lilt.

"H.B. told us you'd be wearing something fantastical. I was absolutely positive you were going to be a magician, so here I am, all dressed up as your assistant."

"Don't listen to her, Jared," voice number two contradicted. "She wouldn't know a magic wand from a swizzle stick. She's a high-wire artist tonight."

"You look lovely," Jared's smooth voice made Sharlie bristle with irritation, though it had a considerably different effect on the woman wearing the costume.

"Thank you," she cooed. "But it's so skimpy, isn't it? I feel positively naked."

"There was considerably more of it before you trashed the cape, darling," the sultry voice proclaimed pointedly.

"Nonetheless," Jared said with a laugh, apparently enjoying the ladies' flirtatious patter, "you look wonderful. You both do," he added diplomatically, sounding revoltingly sincere to Sharlie's itching ears. "What are you dressed up as, Charmaine...a belly dancer?"

Jared's voice fell to a sexy rumble that was matched by Charmaine's own feline purr. Sharlie's hooves started to twitch.

"Not at all, darling," Charmaine murmured. "I opted for something much more romantic. I'm a gypsy. Care to have your immediate future told?"

Jared murmured something low in reply, and Sharlie couldn't make out the words. Stuck as the back end of a quadruped while Jared flirted with a girl named Charmaine, who wore gypsy dresses, Sharlie's fury knew no bounds.

Foretell this, she thought, snapping a kick at Jared's calf.

He grunted.

"Are you all right in there?" The high-wire artist queried with touching concern.

"Oh, fine," Jared reassured. "These heavy horse costumes are sometimes hard to control."

He got another kick.

"It must be horribly warm in there. Why don't I get you something long and cool to sip, you poor baby."

Kick.

"Actually," Jared gritted through a jaw clamped against the pain, "I was just heading that way myself."

"Yes, we saw you stumbling around before we said hello. However do you move your caboose?"

Kick.

"It isn't easy," Jared muttered.

Kick. Kick.

"Is there somebody back there?" That was from the high-wire artist.

"Of course there's someone back there, Ginger," Charmaine scowled. "You think he'd be kicking himself? Who is that, Jared?"

"A very thirsty friend. Ladies, it's been lovely, and, as always, you are lovely." He braced himself to feel a hoof, but apparently Sharlie was resting. "I'm afraid we have to gallop along now," he quipped, pulling Sharlie toward the refreshment table. If he ever caught H.B., hooves would really fly. Flirting with other women wasn't getting the girl, it was getting him pummeled. The mere fact that he had allowed H.B. to talk him into accepting a unicorn costume suggested that he should be wearing the tail end, not Sharlie.

He sighed heavily as he loped through the room. Traffic around the refreshment table was congested, to say the least. Ruby must have invited everyone in the county. He caught sight of his redheaded friend standing near the champagne punch.

"Hang on, Sharlie," he said into the depths of the costume, "we're about to be rescued." He moved next to Ruby and nudged her with the nose of the unicorn head. "Ruby?"

The beautiful redhead turned. She was dressed and made up to look like a harlequin. Blue and green sparkles were painted in curlicues on her cheeks, and her red lips parted in a huge grin as she peered into the unicorn's mesh eyes.

"Jared?"

"Yes, it's me . . . us." His voice was a weary complaint. "Help me get us out of here, will you?"

"Who's in there with you?"

"Sharlie."

"Oh."

Sharlie stood impatiently while Jared and Ruby began untying and removing parts of the costume. When they got to her end, she felt like a baby chick that had finally poked through the shell. She shook her head to clear it and blinked.

When her eyes adjusted to the light, the first thing she saw was Ruby, resplendent in the harlequin outfit, studying her quizzically.

"How long have you been in there?" Ruby asked, her voice laced with laughter and sympathy.

"Too long," Sharlie responded, grumpy despite her desire to be pleasant to their hostess. Jared was standing slightly behind Ruby, the unicorn head tucked under one arm. Sharlie's spirit felt leaden.

First the high-wire artist and the gypsy, and now Ruby. It was too much. Sharlie's enthusiasm for the evening was almost gone. Perhaps she simply didn't possess the competitive spirit necessary to beat these other women back in the battle for Jared's affections. Right now all she wanted was a tall, cool drink.

"So, whose idea was the unicorn costume?" Ruby asked.

"Jared's," Sharlie said, her tone gravely accusatory as she reached for a glass of pale pink punch. Ruby shot a look of query at Jared. Jared rolled his eyes and shrugged.

Pressing her red lips together to keep from laughing, Ruby handed a glass of punch to her neighbor and friend. She had known Jared and his family for years, and throughout those years she had been aware of a certain disconcerting nonchalance in Jared's attitude toward the women he dated and toward the women who flirted with him. Jared had always managed to flirt back, of course, but there was a casual, almost detached quality to his banter that telegraphed to Ruby a lack of profound interest in the proceedings. Unfortunately the women involved rarely caught on as quickly.

Ruby's eyes narrowed in speculation. With Sharlie the situation appeared to be reversed. Jared's interest in the girl had been apparent the evening they "ran into" Sharlie and her very young dinner companion at the Haute Grill, a coincidence Ruby hadn't bought for a minute. She was going to have to corner Jared some time this evening and bully a confession out of him.

"Come on, Sharlie," Ruby said companionably. "I'll show you where you can freshen up. After spending so much time stuck in that stuffy old thing, you can probably use a minute or two to relax."

"Well...thank you." As Sharlie let herself be propelled along by Ruby, she wondered whether she would be able to speak to Jared face-to-face this evening.

Ruby guided her up a lovely curving staircase that would have made her feel like Scarlett O'Hara, if only Sharlie had been garbed in a hoop skirt instead of two hooves and a tail.

As the two women walked down a beautifully appointed hallway, Ruby directed Sharlie into a bathroom, the sheer size of which was breathtaking. The carpet was an exquisite tapestry pattern in shades of cream, celery green and rose. There was a lighted vanity that ran the length of one long wall, and a built-in étagère, attractively stocked with elegant perfume bottles and delicate figurines.

Ruby pulled out the chair in front of the vanity and motioned Sharlie to take a seat. Sharlie obeyed, and Ruby said, "Let's repair some of the damage that costume did."

Sharlie looked at the mirror and grimaced. She looked as hot and sticky as she felt.

Ruby laughed at her expression. "That's not a great costume if you've just had your hair done," she commiserated.

"It's not a great costume, period," Sharlie agreed wryly.

Ruby opened a drawer and began extracting brushes, hair combs and makeup bottles. "I wonder why he picked it out?" she mused.

"Because they were all out of Antony and Cleopatra."

Ruby laughed. "Jared dressed as Antony—now that I'd like to see. And it would have been a much more romantic choice, don't you think?"

Sharlie shrugged and brushed lint off the red T-shirt she wore under the costume. "I suppose so."

"And a lot more fun," Ruby continued. "How did he expect the two of you to dance in that getup? The only thing you could have danced together is the conga." She shook her head. "I must say, Sharlie, you're a much better sport than I would have been. I don't think he ever could have got me into that thing."

Sharlie stared at Ruby's reflection in the mirror. With Ruby he never would have tried. Feminine perfection, that was what the lovely woman represented: it was in her home, in her clothing, in the long, graceful line of her impeccably manicured hands.

Sharlie shook her head. If she remembered to use polish remover before her nail polish peeled off completely, she considered herself a step ahead of the game.

She sighed. For all her efforts this summer, she could never be a Ruby or the gypsy seductress. She was still just Sharlie, and Sharlie, under other circumstances, would have enjoyed arguing over who got to wear the head.

With this realization came a surprising sense of calm. She could stop struggling now. She couldn't turn herself into Ruby, but she and Jared had spent some wonderful times together this summer.

"Well, Sharlie, what do you say?"

Sharlie came up out of her reverie to see Ruby standing over her, eyeshadow, mascara and lip pencil in hand. The woman smiled. "I'm a whiz at repair."

Sharlie smiled back. "Thanks," she said. "But I think I'll just wash up and fix my hair a bit."

"Okay." Ruby didn't seem offended in the least, and Sharlie was glad. She did admire the woman. "If you need anything, feel free to help yourself," Ruby told her.

Sharlie agreed, and Ruby went back downstairs.

When she had finished freshening up, and her hair was scrunched into a thick, wavy cap, Sharlie relaxed a moment and tried to imagine herself as mistress of these surroundings. She would not feel truly comfortable in a house like this, she decided. Given a few minutes and free rein in the house, Lotty would have every piece of downstairs furniture tested for its play appeal.

Spying a stray water drop on the rose marble sink, Sharlie hastily wiped it away. No, she'd be nervous twenty-four hours a day if she had to run this house. She'd rather start in a small place, a cottage, perhaps, with a couple of bedrooms and a breakfast nook that caught the morning light. There would be a cozy hideaway, where she would sneak off to draw, and a simple country kitchen, where she would prepare meals with herbs from her own garden. And a library—there would be a wonderful wood-paneled library with a fireplace.

Sharlie smiled at her own dreams. It sounded like a very simple life, eons away from the elegance and full social life this stately home suggested. And, she imagined, the gypsy and the high-wire artist would be bored just hearing about it. Would any man want to share such domestic simplicity? Sharlie wondered, then shrugged. The right man would.

Heading downstairs to rejoin the party, she heard H.B. call her name. Wasting no time, he took her arm and led her to a quiet corner of the large ballroom.

"I was appalled when Ruby told me that Jared put you in a horse outfit." He launched immediately into a well-rehearsed tirade.

"Unicorn," Sharlie corrected.

H.B. waved one dark-gloved hand. He was costumed as the legendary Valentino. "Whatever. The point is, Jared is an unforgivable oaf, and I have the perfect way to get back at him."

H.B.'s eyes were aglow with enthusiasm. It seemed to Sharlie that, thus far, H.B. was enjoying his grand plan a heck of a lot more than she was.

"I don't want to pay him back," Sharlie dismissed. "And I'm not having much fun trying to make him jealous, either. Nothing personal," she added quickly.

H.B. started to protest, intent on convincing Sharlie that what Jared needed was a good jolt to shock him into awareness.

Sharlie listened with half an ear and even less interest, her attention now focused on the object of H.B.'s new scheme. Jared was standing on the other side of the room, and his system appeared to be receiving all the stimuli it could handle at the moment. Charmaine and Ginger were vying for his attention in the most blatant manner. Even their body language was talking dirty.

Sharlie stared in disbelief. They were so obvious, those two. Was that really what Jared wanted? Her eyes shifted to the man with the unicorn head tucked under his arm, and almost immediately she had her answer: he was bored.

There was a benign but fixed smile on his face. He nodded now and then and added a few words to the conversation, but he wasn't really present.

The awareness gripped Sharlie with a bittersweet tug. She knew him that well. She knew when his eyes were filled with interest and enjoyment and when he would rather be elsewhere. And she knew with a certainty that rocked her that Jared had never wished himself elsewhere when he was with her.

A soft smile rose from her heart and lent a curve to her lips. She didn't possess the particular attributes Charmaine had to offer, but when rubber met the road, Jared was drawn to Sharlie. And that was a sweet secret she could hold on to.

H.B. nudged her on the shoulder. "What are you smiling at?" he complained petulantly. "You haven't even been listening."

"I'd like more punch. Would you care for a glass?"

H.B. looked momentarily contrite. "I'm sorry, I should have asked you. You stay here. I'll get it."

"Thank you, H.B." Sharlie smiled, but as soon as H.B. turned away, she returned her attention to the little group across the room.

The two women were still chattering, but the dark head was lifted, and Sharlie found herself staring directly into Jared's unwavering gaze. Neither party overtly acknowledged the other, but neither looked away. They simply stared, without comment and without inhibition.

It was Jared who broke the contact, and only then did Sharlie notice Ruby's presence at his side. She had come to rescue him. She spoke a few words, and in the next moment he excused himself from Charmaine and Ginger and followed the redhead out of the room.

"I brought you champagne. The punch looked vile." H.B. handed her a fluted glass. "How anybody can ingest anything that pink is beyond me. You do like champagne, don't you? Sharlie? Sharlie!"

"What? Yes, thank you," she murmured, accepting the glass automatically. She had no intention of ever touching the stuff again. "Go on with what you were saying, H.B."

"About the punch? Oh, my plan! Yes, well..." H.B. droned on. Sharlie didn't listen at all. She simply heard his voice, like a backdrop for her own thoughts.

There was a persistent, dull ache inside her. The sweet-sad throb of yearning. The bubbles rose and burst in her champagne and brought with them memories of her first introduction to champagne and to Jared. The pain she had experienced that night bore no resemblance to her feelings now. She loved Jared. Not like a girl, not even like a woman. She was simply Sharlie, in love with Jared and knowing with certainty that he felt something for her in return.

Sharlie's attention didn't waver from her own thoughts until Ruby reappeared, sans Jared. They had been gone a considerable length of time, particularly as Ruby was the hostess of the party. Their extended absence was disturbing enough, but what bothered Sharlie more was that fifteen minutes after Ruby's return, Jared was still nowhere to be seen.

"Well, obviously you're not thirsty, and you're not interested in my great plans, so how about something to eat? The buffet looked rather good." With a mix of resignation and amusement H.B. tried once again to draw Sharlie's attention.

Sharlie looked at H.B. and blinked. "Fine."

H.B. nodded. "Fine," he repeated sardonically. "I'll take this," he said, reaching for Sharlie's champagne. "I can use it. Wait here. I'll bring you a plate, which you won't touch."

He headed for the buffet table, and Sharlie breathed a sigh of relief. She sat down next to a potted fern. The bottom half of the unicorn costume was still held in place with suspenders, and she had to move the tail to avoid sitting on it. She allowed her gaze to meander absently around the room. There was a band at the far end of the long ballroom, and many of the costumed guests had claimed a section of the pegged and grooved floor as a dance space.

Sharlie crossed her legs and swung a hoof to the music.

"Will you dance with me?"

The warm voice came from a distance above her. Sharlie's foot stilled, and she lifted her head. Jared was smiling down at her with that warm, cockeyed grin that made her heart leap.

She started to answer yes immediately, then remembered H.B., and her conscience claimed her. Her fingers fluttered in the direction of the buffet table. "H.B. went—"

"He won't mind," Jared interrupted, the expression in his eyes willing Sharlie to forget the other man and to come with him. He held out his hand, and Sharlie was helpless to resist, the chance to simply put her hand in his too tempting to deny.

She reached out and they touched. His hand was steady and warm as it squeezed hers, gently pulling her to her feet. She was so aware of Jared beside her that the mere act of walking to the dance floor together seemed intimate somehow, and private. When they reached the other couples, Jared lifted the hand that held Sharlie's and turned her toward him. They looked at each other a moment, Sharlie wondering as she gazed at him how a face could have become so dear and so exciting all at once. She felt as though they were the only two people in the room.

Jared put his free hand on her back, wrapping his arm around her and drawing her close. After a moment his other hand released hers, and it, too, curved around her back. Sharlie's own hands crept up to touch his shoulders, and as he pulled her closer, she turned her cheek to rest it on his chest. Wherever they touched, his fingers on her back, her cheek on his chest, her skin burned. They danced slowly. Sharlie's body moved as in a dream. She had no idea how long they danced, she knew only that here in his arms she *felt* that he loved her, and she wanted the feeling to go on forever.

Above her head Sharlie heard Jared's words, so softly uttered she thought she might have imagined them.

"I'll miss you when you go, Sharlie."

She lifted her head to see him, to make sure he really had spoken, but before her eyes could meet his, Jared lowered his head. The moment she had created in her mind over and over for days was happening at last. Jared was kissing her, not like a friend and not like a brother. His lips were warm and firm and the pressure didn't stay subtle this time, it deepened to leave no doubt that he was kissing her like a lover.

Sharlie would never be able to account for the moments that followed the kiss. They were suspended in time. There was no thought and no movement. There was only feeling, and the feeling was indescribable.

The words that broke the connection were completely out of tune with the moment, and they were spoken by an intruder. "Sorry to drag you off the dance floor, Sharlie, but there's a call for you. It sounds fairly important." To Sharlie, Ruby's pleasant voice sounded like metal scraping metal. "You can take it in my room."

Ruby gave her directions to a bedroom that was next to the little dressing room where Sharlie had freshened up. Sharlie barely heard her. *Make her go away,* Sharlie pleaded silently to Jared. The moment was too new, too long-anticipated to relinquish it already.

And as it turned out, it was too elusive as well. Jared's shuttered, expressionless face suggested that their kiss, the touch of his hands might never have happened at all. He gave her the barest echo of a smile and a nod and, with that meager sustenance, sent her off to answer her phone call.

Sharlie moved in soporific slow motion up the stairs and into Ruby's bedroom. Confusion and disappointment were fogging her brain, and when she saw the receiver lying off the hook on the end table, she lifted it without wondering who would call her at Ruby's—or why.

"Hello." She spoke dully into the mouthpiece.

"Sharlie, is that you? For goodness' sake, speak up when someone calls you long distance."

"Aunt Esther?" Sharlie's brows lifted with surprise, then sank rapidly into a frown as the familiar voice barked and cracked over the wires. "What happened? What's wrong?"

"I've talked to you one time all summer and that was when you called to ask for a chicken recipe. Why does there have to be something wrong for me to call my niece?"

"You hate to talk on the phone." Sharlie's frown dropped another centimeter. "And you certainly wouldn't have called here unless there was something specific that you needed. Now tell me what it is."

"Have you had a nice summer? Have you met any decent men?"

"I've been writing you once a week. You know I've had a nice summer."

"What about the men?"

"One or two," Sharlie hedged. After the fiasco with Glen, she certainly wasn't going to give Esther an excuse to send Jared any surprise packages.

"Good!" Her aunt sounded thrilled by the prospect of men in Sharlie's life. "Anyone serious?"

It was hard to know how to answer that one. Sharlie decided on a noncommittal monosyllable to which Esther gave her characteristic grunt of disapproval. "You've had three months. Do you look pretty?"

After a summer of self-discovery, Sharlie doubted the merits of the question, but when she thought of herself in her red T-shirt and unicorn bottom, she grinned.

"Stunning. Now, Aunt Esther, tell me why you called—really."

"It's nothing serious. A little fracture."

"A little what? What did you fracture?"

"It's nothing. Just my leg. It's a clean break . . . I think."

Alarm began its stealthy creep into Sharlie's system. "What do you mean 'you think'? What did the doctor say?"

"I haven't been yet. I hate doctors. Besides, it just happened yesterday."

"Yesterday? Aunt Esther!" Sharlie closed her eyes and told herself to remain calm and coherent. "Aren't you in pain?"

"Tremendous, but I'm getting used to it. I took a couple of aspirin."

"Where's Beverly?" Sharlie decided to speak to the reasonable woman who had been working with her aunt while Sharlie was away. "Put Beverly on the phone."

"I gave her the week off. Her niece is getting married in Dallas. I couldn't deny her the joy of seeing her only niece get married at the age of twenty-two. How old are you now?''

Sharlie counted to ten. "All right, listen, what about Mac?" She named a friend with whom her aunt regularly played cards. "Can he come over and take you to the doctor tonight?"

"I suppose so," Esther wavered. "Although, he's no spring chicken. He's probably asleep already," she grumbled disgustedly.

Sharlie held the phone to her shoulder for a moment and shook her head. She had painfully few options. Returning the phone to her ear, she spoke with what she hoped was calm assertiveness. "Call Mac. Have him take you to the emergency room at Hoag Hospital. It's very close to you. Then ask him if he can stay with you until tomorrow. I should be there by noon."

"I don't want you to do that."

"I'll be there by noon," Sharlie repeated firmly.

"Okay, if I can't talk you out of it."

"You can't. I love you very much, and I'm glad you called me. You do as I asked, all right?"

"Yes, I will. And you drive safely. And don't worry about getting here by noon. Anytime tomorrow will be fine. Just get a good night's rest."

Sharlie agreed. They each blew a kiss into the phone, and rang off. Sharlie sank to the bed with her head in her hands. It looked like the party was over—in spades.

On the southern end of the line, in her little cottage in Laguna, Esther placed the phone in its cradle and sat back in her favorite recliner. She pulled the lever on the right, and the foot rest came up. She lifted her left foot, wriggled it, and put it back on the rest. Then she lifted her right foot, wriggled, and returned it to the rest. She gave one final, good stretch, smiled and settled in. All she had to do now was wait for Sharlie to return.

* * *

Instead of heading for her apartment above the catering shop, Sharlie went straight to Esther's cottage when she exited the freeway in Orange County and turned onto Laguna Canyon Road. She was grateful for the scenic drive. The gentle landscape helped her to relax and collect her tumbling thoughts before she faced Aunt Esther.

Lotty was wide awake and restless in the seat beside her, as she had been almost since they left Big Sur at five o'clock that morning. Lotty hadn't wanted to leave any more than Sharlie had. Every dozen miles or so, a mournful howl would be emitted from the tiny body. It was a sound Sharlie could have done without; it merely amplified her own dismay.

Even now she wasn't sure what she had expected when she'd left Ruby's bedroom and had gone to tell Jared that she was leaving. What had she wanted? An argument? A show of regret? An offer to accompany her?

Yes. All of the above would have been nice.

Any of the above.

She would have appreciated some sign that her leaving was going to affect him in a way that was more than casual. She wanted that indication and a promise that he would not let her go for long, that they would be together again soon.

What she hadn't expected was that neither he nor H.B. would be anywhere in sight and that she would be forced to take a cab home. To add insult to injury, when he did return to the inn, Jared seemed more chagrined that Sharlie had been forced to take a cab than he was dismayed over the prospect of her leaving. The businesslike tone he maintained during their brief conversation still frustrated and confused her. How could he be so intense, so romantic one moment and so utterly blasé the next?

"I feel really awful about leaving you on such short notice," she told him. "If you need me to stay a couple of days, I'm sure I could work something out. My aunt—"

"No, no. Not at all. We'll be fine." Jared reassured her so decisively that Sharlie felt as useful as Confederate bills. "The season is winding down. I'll talk to Mrs. Manzer. She can always bring someone in from an agency for a couple of weeks, if she needs to."

"Yes, she told me you do that occasionally. Well, if you're sure."

"Absolutely. Your contract was almost up. You would have been leaving soon, anyway. You just look after your aunt. She must need you now." He smiled. It was a kind, impersonal smile.

Sharlie nodded. "Yes."

She smacked the heel of her hand on the steering wheel. In the face of Jared's nonchalance, she hadn't had the courage to mention their kiss or to ask if they would see each other again. They had simply said their goodbyes, and Sharlie had packed the memories of her summer into her little suitcase. Sleep had eluded her, so by five the following morning, she and Lotty were on the road to home.

"Oh, please, give me a break here," Sharlie wailed as her traveling companion sent up another heart-rending howl. "Look, we're right here," she cajoled, pulling the car into Esther's short, brick driveway. "Be good. I'll sneak you something to eat."

Tucking Lotty under her arm, Sharlie went to the front door and gave her hair a quick comb-through with her fingers before she let herself into her aunt's cottage.

"Aunt Esther!" Sharlie hollered into the house. Silence was her only answer. Frowning, Sharlie hitched a squirming Lotty higher in her arms and walked into the small living room her aunt had packed with antiques.

"Aunt Esther?" she called again, then spied her diminutive aunt in the meticulously pruned English garden that lay beyond double French doors.

Mouth agape as she watched her aunt, Sharlie stepped into the yard. "What are you doing?"

"Cutting back the—" Esther started to answer, but before she finished, she turned her silvery head, and her blue eyes blinked in surprise.

"You're home nice and early."

Sharlie's eyes narrowed on her aunt. There was no cast, no ace bandage, no evidence of an injury anywhere on Esther's body. At the moment, in fact, her legs were neatly tucked under her while she knelt by the snapdragons.

Following the path of her niece's thoughts, Esther smiled blandly and offered an explanation. "That doctor told me exercise would be good for my leg. I see you brought your cat. Please don't put her down. Last time she ate three primroses."

"Aunt Esther, what happened to your broken leg?"

"It's not a break, after all," Esther said happily. "Isn't that lovely? I was having muscle spasms. You get them at my age." She waved a gloved hand at Sharlie. "Nothing to worry about."

Sharlie stared at her aunt in disbelief. "You were having muscle spasms?" Incomprehension filled her expression and her voice. "Why didn't you let me know? I left those people at a moment's notice with no chef. It was the worst possible timing!" Sharlie's frustration momentarily obliterated her relief at finding Esther well. "Why didn't you call me back?"

"I got home from the emergency room too late. I didn't want to wake you. Besides, I met a nice young man there, a doctor. I think we should take him some brownies to say thank you for saving my mobility. He's single."

Sharlie pushed her hand through her hair and tried to quell her exasperation. Esther was fine and that was the important thing. But the knowledge that leaving Jared so abruptly hadn't been necessary at all made her quiver with frustration.

"Are you able to work?" she asked her aunt, struggling for a sense of calm.

Esther shook the dirt off her cotton gardening gloves. "Well, I should rest. I'm not as young as I used to be."

"You're sure you're all right?" Sharlie probed, residual concern sneaking back. "I've never heard you talk that way before."

"I'm fine. I'm going to rest for a couple of days, not go into retirement!" Esther snapped, her feisty spirit rising to the forefront, as always.

Sharlie sighed. "Did we lose any business?"

"No, but the next couple of days might be busy." Esther's acute blue eyes were leveled at Sharlie from under her straw hat. "You look pretty with your hair lighter. But your letters were boring." She sniffed disapprovingly. "Come into the kitchen. I'll make you a sandwich, and you'll tell me something interesting. I hope."

With an agility that belied her trouble with muscle spasms, Esther rose to her feet, collected her clippings and trotted to the house. "Bring the cat."

When Sharlie was home again in her own little apartment above the catering shop, she sat on the couch, propped her feet on the coffee table, and thought about the inconsistencies of the afternoon. For someone with spasms so severe that she thought her leg was broken, Esther had been remarkably spry and pain free this afternoon. There had been no need for Sharlie to rush home. She could have stayed the morning, at least.

Pursing her lips, Sharlie hauled Lotty onto her lap and nuzzled her fur. Lotty squirmed. After her confinement in the car, she wanted to play, not snuggle. Sharlie let her go. Cuddling Lotty was great, but it wasn't what she wanted right now, either. She sighed. Love was a lot like butter: there was no substitute for the real thing. What she needed was someone to scratch *her* behind the ears.

She touched her fingers to her lips and closed her eyes. That kiss had been everything she had dreamed a kiss would be. Her foolish, romantic heart would have that gratification at least, the memory of that kiss.

Sharlie put her feet down on the floor and sat up. She was doing it again. She was giving up, waiting for life to come and get her, instead of going out and grabbing it herself. If she experienced passion once, she could experience it again. That was no goodbye kiss Jared had given her. If he kissed her with passion once, he could do it again. Passion was not portion controlled, after all. With a little courage, she could ask for a second helping.

With resolution filling her heart, Sharlie marched to the phone. Her hand grew more and more clammy with each ring until Mrs. Manzer's pleasant voice chirped on the other end of the line.

"Sharlie!" the woman exclaimed happily after Sharlie announced herself. "We miss you already."

They chatted for several moments until Sharlie gathered the nerve to ask to speak with Jared. Mrs. Manzer hesitated.

"He's gone away for a couple of days. His sister and brother-in-law are in Orange County, and he went to see them. I think they're in your area, in fact. I could give you the name and number of his hotel. He'd love to talk to you, I'm sure."

Sharlie rapidly declined. Jared had known he was going to be mere minutes away from her, and he had chosen not to inform her of the fact. Suddenly she wished with all her might that she had not phoned the inn today. She tried to ring off as casually as possible, but her hurt must have been evident, because Mrs. Manzer's voice became so soothing and maternal in tone that Sharlie could almost feel the woman's hand patting her on the head.

"You know what?" Mrs. Manzer said. "I'll just bet he plans to call you while he's down there. He said he didn't know how long he'd be away. I'm sure you'll be hearing from him in a day or two." She sounded so satisfied with her logic that there was nothing for Sharlie to do but agree and say goodbye.

Sharlie worked hard the rest of the day, pummeling the bread dough and grating carrots with enough force to turn them into carrot juice. Her frustration didn't abate, but at least it had an outlet. At six-thirty, she closed the shop and drove to Balboa Island to walk as fast and as far as she could. She wanted to be too exhausted to think. She covered the entire island twice, striding first by the bay, and then zigzagging up and down the network of streets that were named after gems. She tried to memorize their order: Amethyst, Sapphire, Pearl; Coral, Ruby, Opal. She chanted to herself as she walked, anything to keep her mind as neutral as possible.

By eight-thirty, when her legs ached and she was too tired to care about anything but a warm bath, she considered that her mission was accomplished, and she headed for her car. The lights along Park Street glittered gaily, and there were still pockets of crowds dotting the small street and filling the island's popular restaurants. Sharlie strolled past Barton's to smell the garlic and to see if she could lift an idea or two from the posted menu. As always there were people cramming the restaurant's small entry.

Sharlie smiled. She wouldn't mind having a restaurant like this one, a place where people dined in simple, uncomplicated elegance. Tonight's diners did not defer to the fact that the island was a casual beach community; they were dressed classically. They didn't seem to mind the wait to be seated, either.

Two particularly well-heeled couples stood chatting and laughing as they waited for the hostess to call their party. The women were lovely in simple, form-fitting dresses that seemed to have jumped off the pages of *Harper's Bazaar* and right into their wardrobes. And the men... Sharlie's mouth fell open as she stared. The men were Glen and Jared.

She darted back behind the wall and peered around for a longer look. She should have recognized the women before. Gina was as lovely now as Sharlie remembered, and Ruby was drawing stares simply by standing there. Sharlie's gaze was glued to the foursome as the hostess arrived to guide them to their table. The couples moved off, Glen and Gina first, followed by Ruby with Jared at her side. His hand was on her bare back.

Sharlie watched the couple stroll merrily into the dining room. Then, without a murmur and without a single expression crossing her face, she turned and walked to her car.

Chapter Twelve

"The Fischers are having another picnic on their dock a week from Saturday, and they want the pasta salad with Japanese eggplant again. It's for six this time. This is their twelfth picnic since June. They must know everyone in Newport Beach."

Esther sat on the stool and read from her list. "Also, the Kandazians called and want to add stuffed grape leaves to the buffet at their daughter's wedding. The couple is going to Greece for their honeymoon. I told her they'd have plenty of grape leaves in Greece, but she said she still wants them." Esther shrugged. "We'll have to buy some pine nuts." Her sharp gaze narrowed at Sharlie. "Are you listening to me?"

Dragging a spoon through a huge bowl of muffin batter, Sharlie nodded. "Eggplant and pine nuts."

"You're going to turn that batter into shoe leather." Esther complained, her lips compressing with exasperation. "What's the matter with you lately? You've been home two days, you don't talk to me, I can't get a word out of you about your summer, and every time I turn around, you're beating up the food.''

Sharlie pulled the spoon from the batter and whacked it soundly on the lip of the bowl. The orange-marmalade muffins were going to taste like rubber.

''Nothing's wrong,'' she said, refusing to offer any explanation that would require her to think of Jared. Since yesterday evening she had kept her mind a blank, except to thank God that she hadn't been able to contact Jared. She had been spared that embarrassment, and she had learned her lesson once and for all. The pain wasn't worth it. Romance must be for the masochistic at heart.

The ride of emotions Jared had taken her on was enough to put her off roller coasters for life. It was going to take every bit of her strength to refrain from indulging in fruitless self-pity.

''Well, if you're not going to talk to me, then I'm going to make new muffins. You work on a picnic basket, that shouldn't take too much concentration.''

''Are the Fischers having another picnic?'' Sharlie mumbled in distraction.

''Not since the one I told you about ten minutes ago!'' Esther grabbed the bowl Sharlie was staring blankly at and dumped the contents into the sink.

''I hope it doesn't clog the pipes,'' she muttered as the glop slithered down the drain. Esther pulled a piece of paper off the bulletin board and slapped it on the counter in front of her niece. ''Here. We got this order last night— from a friend of yours, I believe. Very romantic. He wanted silk roses on the basket. Wait till you see it. I made it beautiful.''

Sharlie glanced lethargically at the work order. ''How do you know he's a friend of mine?''

Esther pulled the paper back and looked at it. ''Jared Wright,'' she read. ''Isn't that the man you worked for this summer?''

Sharlie grabbed the slip. "Yes."

"So what am I, senile? You think I can't remember a simple name?"

Sharlie's expression was grim. Jared had called. To order a picnic basket. "When is he picking it up?"

"He's not. He wants it delivered to his hotel suite." Esther turned to rinse out the sink. "So, is he a nice man, this Jared?"

"He's okay."

"Okay? That's it?" She frowned. "He is single, isn't he?"

The breath Sharlie was holding was expelled on a hiss. "Yes, he's single. He's single, he's handsome, he makes a good living, and he's intelligent. And I'm not interested."

Esther pursed her pink-slicked lips. "Well, that makes good sense. Make sure you get the basket to him by six." Turning the bowl upside down on the counter so it would dry, she took herself into her office at the back of the shop and closed the door.

Sharlie stared at the work order, and Jared's name leapt out at her. It was too galling. She was supposed to make the basket and deliver it so that Jared could share a romantic picnic with Ruby? Of all the unmitigated arrogance. So she was still nothing more than his cook.

Men were all alike, really. They were truly decent human beings only when their hormones were on the inactive list. Once their little ears perked up and they sensed a woman, they would do anything to reassure themselves that they possessed a proper dose of machismo. They'd even kiss you until you believed they were capable of sincerity and human emotion.

Sharlie's jaw clenched until the muscle showed. She would not provide sustenance for Jared's lustful endeavors. It wasn't enough that he'd had Charmaine and Ginger . . . and Sharlie . . . swooning at his feet the other night. Tonight he needed more, he needed . . . different. A tear escaped the hand that was scrubbing like a windshield wiper across her cheek. Catering other people's romances was getting to be a habit.

Well, fortunately she had already declared her personal independence from all forms of slavish devotion to romantic ideals. She would tell him precisely where he could take his picnic. She would refuse the order; let them eat fast food like everybody else. She would—

Sharlie raised the slip of paper she held in her hand. Her fingers curled into a fist, and the light of determination fired her eyes. She would make the food. She would deliver the basket. It would be a picnic they wouldn't soon forget.

Later in the evening of that same day, Sharlie stared into the contents of her refrigerator. It was eight o'clock, two hours after she had delivered the picnic basket to Jared's room at the Four Seasons Newport. Actually, *deliver* was inaccurate. Rather, it was two hours after she had dropped the basket in the hall, knocked on his door, and had run like a thief in the night. For the past hour and a half she had been contemplating a binge of mammoth proportions.

Ruby and Jared must have tasted the food in the basket by now, but Sharlie didn't want to think about that. She gazed at the butter, wondering what she could eat with it.

A loud pounding on the shop door jarred her into alertness. She closed the refrigerator and listened. When the knocking sounded again, she crept to the door to inch aside the shade.

The glow from the street lamp shone on mahogany hair and amber eyes that sparkled brilliantly in the dark night. There was neither anger nor pleasure in the eyes when they met Sharlie's, there was merely a gleam of determination. Jared pointed to the doorknob.

"Would you open the door, please? There is a police officer coming up the block, and he's staring at me strangely."

Sharlie dropped the shade and moved to the drawer where she kept the key to the door. Her hands were shaking, and she felt a thousand butterflies beating against her tummy. She willed them to stop.

When she unlocked the door, Jared strode in without pause. He was wearing a tuxedo that was molded to his shoulders and which made him appear as darkly and formally handsome as he was on the night they'd first met. If not for the loosened tie and unfastened top buttons of his dress shirt, it would have been difficult to picture this gentleman as the Jared with whom she had argued and played softball and read children's books. But it was Jared. He was here now, and dangling from his hand was the flowered picnic basket Sharlie had left in the hall.

Sharlie pushed at her bangs and tugged at the oversized, magenta Minnie Mouse T-shirt that now covered her jeans. She smiled weakly. "If I'd known you were coming, I would have dressed."

Jared plopped the basket onto the counter. "I didn't know I was coming. In fact, after you dropped the basket off—and I can only assume it was you, since you didn't wait for me to answer the door—I thought I wouldn't be seeing you at all."

He looked at her accusingly, his handsome face stern, and Sharlie shifted. Five minutes away, and he hadn't planned to seek her out at all on this trip. She shrugged to hide her hurt and her anger.

"Well, you're busy. I'm busy."

Jared indicted her with a look. "Too busy to wait for me to come to the door? Too busy to say hello to a friend?" He shook his handsome head. "No, I don't think so. Not if we really were friends." He leaned his elbows on the counter. "So that made me wonder. Maybe Sharlie doesn't want to be friends, I thought. Maybe her feelings aren't friendly."

He raised a brow in question, throwing the ball into Sharlie's court, and she didn't know quite what to do with it.

"You didn't come to see me, either."

186 MR. WRIGHT

"Ah! But I knew I'd be seeing you when you delivered the basket. Were you offended that I didn't speak with you myself?"

"No, of course not," Sharlie scoffed. "I told you, I've been busy since I've been back, and I didn't wait for you to answer the door because I didn't want to intrude on you and Ruby."

Jared straightened up and frowned. "Ruby?"

He seemed genuinely puzzled, and Sharlie remembered that unless she admitted to seeing them together at Barton's she shouldn't have known that Jared was with Ruby tonight. She scrambled to cover her tracks.

"I'm sorry. Weren't you with Ruby? When I saw the basket, I just assumed it was for her. The two of you seemed so close."

Jared's frown deepened a moment, then his brow cleared with understanding, and he smiled a small, inward smile. "No, it wasn't for Ruby. It was for a a different young lady."

"A different one?" Sharlie allowed the censure to drip off her words. "Busy, busy."

"Yes," Jared nodded, looking pensive. "But she stood me up." He put his hand in his pockets and shook his head. "You know, I think I know now how you felt about Glen."

"Do you?"

Jared nodded. "I've given you some bad advice. I told you to play dating games. That's what I did with this woman, and it didn't work."

He shook his head ruefully. "I did everything wrong. I enlisted the help of friends. I tried clever little stratagems. I did everything but tell her how I feel." He looked like he wanted to kick himself, and his voice dropped to a low, ingenuous confession. "And I think I've known how I felt about her from almost the first moment I saw her."

Sharlie felt her body tremor. "Why didn't you tell her?"

"Because I wasn't positive she was interested. And I was afraid to believe what I thought I saw, because I've never wanted anything so much in my life as to be the right person for her. So I tried everything but honesty, the one thing that might have worked."

Sharlie saw the yearning and the question in his eyes, and it amazed her. "Because you were afraid of being hurt?" she whispered.

Jared nodded. He pulled something out of his pocket. "But rejection is such a little thing when a lifetime stands in front of you."

He looked down, and Sharlie, who hadn't taken her eyes off his face before now, saw that he was turning a small gray velvet box over in his hands.

"You should have seen the elaborate lengths I went to for tonight." His mouth curved self-mockingly. "I had her aunt call up and pretend to need her at home. And then, because I was nervous and I wanted everything to be absolutely right, I gathered moral support. I had a friend help me decorate a hotel suite and plan the whole scene. I told everyone but the lady in question what I had planned. You see, I had this great idea for a romantic picnic." He shook his head. "Elaborate lengths."

He opened the gray box and pulled a delicate, antique gold and emerald ring from the velvet cushion. Jared's eyes met hers openly, honestly, with no secrets and with nothing hidden or saved. She could read a world of love in his eyes, and she gazed back with her heart shining clearly in hers.

"I adore you, Sharlie Kincaid. And if you'll let me, I'll love you for the rest of our lives."

Her eyes sparkled, and she shook her head in pure wonderment. "I think this is better than any of my dreams. And I dream big. I love you, Jared."

He put the ring on her finger, and their lips met to close all distance between them. Their kiss was as magical and romantic and unrestrained as either had ever hoped a kiss would be, and it was finally, utterly real.

When they pulled away, it was only slightly, and Jared bent his head to whisper in Sharlie's ear. "I hope your aunt won't mind adding a wedding to her calender. But first I'm going to give you that courtship you missed."

Sharlie returned his cuddle. "The heck with the courtship. I know you're the right man for me. Marry me first, and then we'll date."

Jared laughed happily. "What will your aunt think?"

"She will be delighted." Sharlie twinkled. It was a definite, delicious understatement.

She kissed Jared again, then pulled back when a new thought struck.

"Wait a minute. Why did you wait so long to come over here tonight? I dropped that basket off at six o'clock sharp." And she had almost eaten herself right out of a wedding gown.

Jared grinned. "When you dumped the basket and ran, I thought it was your characteristically subtle way of telling me to get lost. I needed time to regroup. I needed a little encouragement."

He nuzzled her ear. Sharlie swooned. Her ear was in heaven. "And how were you encouraged?"

"I got hungry."

"I don't get it."

He nibbled on her earlobe. "Your pâté was a little on the spicy side. Reminded me of a wedding cake I once had. But my suspicions were confirmed when I tasted the lobster salad. Only someone who truly cared would make something that awful. Right?"

Sharlie closed her eyes and nodded, delighted to confess as she basked in the sensations his lips were creating. "You're very perceptive."

"Your pâté was hideous."

Sharlie giggled as his nose tickled her. "Secret family recipe. It's been handed down for generations."

"And the lobster salad?" His lips moved down her neck.

"Jalapeño juice," she murmured, loving every moment of what he was doing to her neck.

"Mmmm. Make it again for our tenth anniversary."

"Whatever you say." She would promise him anything.

"And our twentieth."

"Absolutely."

"And our thirtieth."

"Oh, yes...."

* * * * *

INTIMATE MOMENTS®
10TH
Anniversary

Celebrate our anniversary with a fabulous collection of firsts....

The first Intimate Moments titles written by three of your favorite authors:

NIGHT MOVES — Heather Graham Pozzessere
LADY OF THE NIGHT — Emilie Richards
A STRANGER'S SMILE — Kathleen Korbel

Silhouette Intimate Moments is proud to present a FREE hardbound collection of our authors' firsts—titles that you will treasure in the years to come, from some of the line's founding writers.

This collection will not be sold in retail stores and is available only through this exclusive offer. Look for details in Silhouette Intimate Moments titles available in retail stores in May, June and July.

You're Invited

Silhouette Romance celebrates June brides and grooms and *You're Invited!* Be our guest as five special couples find the magic ingredients for happily-*wed*-ever-afters! Look for these wonderful stories by some of your favorite authors...

WED

Silhouette
R O M A N C E™

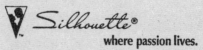